BEACON STREET GIRLS

This book belongs to:

VERITAS AMICITIA GAUDIUM
truth friendship fun!

Who's Who

BSG

Katani Summers
a.k.a. Kgirl ... Katani has a strong fashion sense and business savvy. She is stylish, loyal & cool.

Avery Madden
Avery is passionate about all sports and animal rights. She is energetic, optimistic & outspoken.

Charlotte Ramsey
A self-acknowledged "klutz" and an aspiring writer, Charlotte is all too familiar with being the new kid in town. She is intelligent, worldly & curious.

Isabel Martinez
Her ambition is to be an artist. She was the last to join the Beacon Street Girls. She is artistic, sensitive & kind.

Maeve Kaplan-Taylor
Maeve wants to be a movie star. Bubbly and upbeat, she wears her heart on her sleeve. She is entertaining, friendly & fun.

Ms. Razzberry Pink
The stylishly pink proprietor of the "Think Pink" boutique is chic, gracious & charming.

Marty
The adopted best dog friend of the Beacon Street Girls is feisty, cuddly & suave.

Happy Lucky Thingy and **alter ego Mad Nasty Thingy**
Marty's favorite chew toy, it is known to reveal its alter ego when shaken too roughly. He is most often happy.

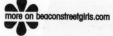

more on beaconstreetgirls.com

BEACON STREET GIRLS

ISBN-13: 978-0-545-11164-5
ISBN-10: 0-545-11164-1

12 11 10 9 8 7 6 5 4 3 2 1   8 9 10 11 12 13/0

Printed in the U.S.A.   40

First Scholastic printing, September 2008

A very special acknowledgement goes to Sara Hoagland Hunter
for her inspirational contribution to the development of the
Beacon Street Girls: Worst Enemies/Best Friends.

Series Editor: Roberta MacPhee
Art Direction: Pamela M. Esty
Book Design: Dina Barsky
Illustration: Pamela M. Esty

BEACON STREET GIRLS

worst enemies/best friends

SCHOLASTIC INC.

New York Toronto London Auckland Sydney
Mexico City New Delhi Hong Kong Buenos Aires

ଔ

This book is dedicated to any girl
who has ever felt like the new girl.

Life is full of surprises
and making mistakes is part of the journey.
So, go for your dreams. Choose wisely.
Stand up for yourselves, be kind to the planet,
and above all, be a good friend.

Enjoy your journey,
Annie Bryant ✿

PART ONE

WORST ENEMIES

ॐ

Charlotte

STARS OVER BEACON STREET

STARS AND BOOKS have always been my best friends. My books go with me wherever we move. And the stars, they are always there when we get there. The first stars I look for are the three in Orion's belt because they're the brightest. Close friends are harder to find. Well, actually, *keeping* them is the hard part. Every time I find a best friend, we move.

The night before starting Abigail Adams Junior High, I pulled my fleece blanket around me and snuggled deep into the beanbag chair I had dragged out on the balcony of my new bedroom. I missed Sophie and Paris, but I was excited, too. This year was going to be different. Dad's a writer and likes to live wherever his book in progress is based. We've moved every two or three years since I was four. For the first time ever, I was the one who had chosen where Dad and I would live: Brookline, Massachusetts, U.S.A. I was born here, and even though I could barely remember it, this was where we were a family before my mother died. I hoped we'd be here for a long, long time ...

"Charlotte? Why is your light out?"

"It's easier to see the stars. I'm outside, Dad."

"Of course. How could I forget!" he said. "Isn't that a great balcony?"

"It's just perfect! Come see!"

Dad came through my bedroom and the outside door to kneel beside me, as he had many times over the years. "Remember the first time I showed you Orion?"

"Sure, Dad ... Africa."

"Little different here, isn't it?" he said, putting his arm around me.

"Yeah ... in the southern hemisphere, Orion's upside down. But you can still see him from here. I like that."

"How are you feeling about school tomorrow?"

"You mean, like in Africa, surrounded by laughing hyenas? Don't worry, Dad. The kids will not be laughing at me tomorrow. No more first-day disasters."

"I'm almost sorry to hear that," said Dad. "It's become kind of a first-night tradition to hear how you shake things up." He smiled. "Which story is my favorite? Port Douglas? No—Paris! Sure I won't be getting a phone call about my daughter spying in the boys' bathroom?"

"Dad, they speak English in this country. How was I supposed to know that 'Garçon' meant boy? I couldn't escape once all those garçons were in there. Tomorrow will be different, you'll see. What about you? How are you feeling about *your* first day of school tomorrow, *Professor* Ramsey?"

"Well, it's been awhile, but I dragged out the old lesson plans, and they're not looking too shabby."

"Lesson plans? Come on, Dad. What are you wearing? That's what they're going to notice." I dragged him inside. "I've been studying kids for a week here to figure out how to fit in. I've got the Brookline camouflage look all figured out ...

hooded sweatshirt, jeans, and flip-flops."

"Charlotte, do you honestly think they're going to care about my clothes after I enchant them with my fascinating thoughts on creative writing? I have gems to share about character development that ..."

"Dad, I hate to tell you this, but kids notice teachers' clothes much more than what they say, especially the first day. I think you should wear jeans. Are you riding your bike?"

"Sure." He nodded.

"Then, whatever you do, don't leave your pants tucked into your socks."

"My daughter, the nerd police," he laughed.

He leaned against the doorway and checked out my room.

"This looks great, Charlotte. That photo you took from the top of the Eiffel Tower is one of my favorites."

He walked over to the desk, which was perfectly arranged with my pens, journals, laptop, and picture of me and Mom on the swan boats in Boston when I was a baby.

"I'm glad you like the desk," he said. "Your mother spent a lot of hours at it, grading papers."

"It's the best!" I said, giving him a hug. "I've always wanted a writing desk with a cool view."

"Are you about ready for bed?"

"I want to send Sophie an email."

"Well, don't stay up too late. Goodnight, sweetheart."

"Night, Dad," I said, giving him a kiss.

To: Sophie
From: Charlotte
Subject: school!

Hey sophie. 2morrow's the 1st day of
school and i'm starting all over again.
i miss you so much. Sooooo glad you got
the pics of our house. i knew you would
love the room on top with all the windows.
fantastique, magnifique, merveilleux,
n'est-ce pas? i call it the Tower. dad
says it's just a decoration. I'm hoping
there's a passageway to a real room. glad
you approve of my new bedroom with the
balcony. a little different than swinging
from a hammock in the houseboat. speaking
of the houseboat, will you check if
Orangina by any chance came home?
Au revoir, charlotte

I didn't want to think anymore about school, so I began
to write an idea for my best-seller book file. If I write fast
enough, I can usually chase away the butterflies zooming
around in my stomach.

New Kid Survival Guide

*About the Author: Charlotte Elizabeth Ramsey has
been new three times in five years in three different
countries. She is the world's leading expert on
embarrassing school moments and writes completely from
her own experience as a disaster magnet. Someday she*

hopes to master the art of fitting in. Charlotte lives with her father, Richard, author of Serengeti Summer ... or How I Survived an Elephant Stampede and Lessons on a Coral Reef ... or The Great White Shark Is Not Your Friend. She used to live with her cat, Orangina, but she ran away the day before Charlotte left Paris.

Chapter One: Top Ten Things NOT to Do the First Day of School
By Someone Who Has Done Them All

1. *Wear a long African skirt while riding your bike to school in Australia.*
2. *Wear underwear with purple pigs on them in case your skirt gets pulled off and eaten by your bike chain.*
3. *Wear shorts if you have hairy legs.*
4. *Introduce yourself in a loud, friendly voice to a group of girls applying eye makeup.*
5. *Bring anything in a Thermos.*
6. *Go to lunch by yourself.*
7. *Eat school porridge.*
8. *Join a conversation about a movie you've never seen.*
9. *Throw up on a cute boy's shoe.*
10. *Eat anything with poppy seeds in it and then smile without checking your teeth in a mirror.*

Even though I was still nervous, I saved the file, shut down my computer, and climbed into bed. After twenty minutes of tossing and turning like a beached codfish, I flipped the light back on. Time for desperate measures. I hopped out of bed and got my oldest stuffed animal, Truffles the Pig, down from the shelf. I also took my Mom's old denim jacket off the back of my desk chair and put it on over my pajamas. I wear it for inspiration when I'm writing, but that night, I needed it for comfort. I pulled it around me and got back into bed, fingering the charm bracelet in the pocket. The bracelet was a baby present from Mom, and while I outgrew it ages ago, I've always kept it. With Truffles beside me and my fleece blanket all snug around me, I began to feel cozy. There was just one last thing I needed to do. I reached for the worn copy of *Charlotte's Web* that was my mother's when she was little. I turned to the last page and read the line Mom had underlined:

> *"It is not often that someone comes along who is a true friend and a good writer. Charlotte was both."*

Then I began reading the story I've read a hundred times since I was little, and in the comfort of the story I knew so well, I fell asleep.

CHAPTER 2

Charlotte

THE BEST EVER

MAYBE I WAS STILL ON PARIS TIME, because I woke before my alarm. The morning sounds here were so different—no gulls, no creak of ropes against the dock, no lapping of waves on the side of the boat. Instead, there were rustling leaves, chirping birds, and from the bottom of the hill, screeching brakes of the Green Line streetcar.

I missed our houseboat, but it sure was nice to have my own bathroom. I looked in the mirror. Oh no. Serious bedhead. It took about thirty seconds to get dressed, but forever to get my stupid hair right. I hoped kids here wore braids. I got my glasses from the bedside table and chose five of my favorite bracelets for good luck: One I had made out of hemp with Sophie, two emerald green malachite bracelets I bought at a market in Tanzania, one made of neon orange plastic from Paris, and, my favorite, a beautiful sea glass charm bracelet from Australia.

Dad is not a morning person. In fact, any time before eight, he pretty much looks as if a herd of elephants slept on his face. That's why I couldn't believe he was up, dressed, and waiting at the kitchen table when I got there.

"Dad! What are you doing up?"

"A toast!" he said, raising his orange juice. "To the two of us! May the first day of school be disaster free and ..."

"May you inspire some student to write a great book, just like you!"

Dad groaned. "A book is like a hot dog. It's a lot better if you don't look too hard at what goes into it ... I can't find your class assignment letter. I had it yesterday—where'd that pile of mail go?"

"Dad, we talked about this. We're keeping mail on the front hall table. Don't worry. I have the letter."

"What would I do without you?" he asked.

"Shuffle about in your pajamas, Dad. Gotta go. I don't want to be the last one into the school."

Dad gave me a hug and said what he always says the first day of school: "Knock 'em dead, kid."

"I hope not, Dad."

WELCOME TO AMERICA

I loved the walk from our house down Corey Hill toward the shops and school. Both sides of the steep street were lined with big trees whose leaves were already turning yellow. I couldn't wait for the street to be lined in gold, orange, and red, like the pictures of New England I'd always seen. A path between two houses led off into the woods. There was still a lot to explore, even at the top of the hill.

The steepness made me pick up speed until I was almost running, and the faster I went, the better I felt. This would be a good day—I was sure of it.

At the bottom of the hill, I turned left onto Beacon, a street that's unlike any I've ever lived on. Green streetcars rattled along steel tracks in the center of the road, with three lanes of traffic on either side. I checked out the windows of a party store full of piñatas and Happy Birthday banners, and walked past the stacked trash cans and ladders at the hardware store.

At the corner, I turned left onto Harvard Street, past a building that looked like a castle. Travel posters in the window advertised trips to Hawaii, Greece, and Egypt. No thanks, I thought. I'm not going anywhere for a long, long time.

I crossed Harvard Street where a big, hairy man in a white apron was arranging fruit outside of his market. I was feeling so good right then, I just couldn't help calling out "Good morning!"

He stopped piling apples and scrunched his bushy eyebrows together.

"For you, maybe," he said gruffly, with a heavy accent.

"Where are you from?" I asked.

"What? You not like the way I speak English?" he asked, picking up an apple.

Grou-chy. "No. Your English is great. It's just, I've lived a lot of places, and I can't figure out your accent."

He polished the apple with a corner of his apron. "If you live so many places, why you never live in Russia?"

I had no idea what to say. "I guess because my father never wrote a book there. What's it like?"

"Terrible," he said with a laugh. "Why else you think I move here?"

"I moved here too," I said. "Just two weeks ago."

"Two weeks? And already your English is almost good as Yuri's? Well done." He tossed me the polished apple. "Welcome to America. You never get better anywhere in the world than a New England Macintosh apple."

"Hey, thanks!" I said.

"Stay out of my way, young lady," he said, eyes twinkling, "and we will be getting along fine."

An odd man, but it was a good apple, tart and crisp. I crunched and munched my way down the street. Everything was fine until I felt a piece of peel caught between my front teeth. I checked my teeth in a bakery window. Not pretty. I picked and pulled with my fingernail. Why wouldn't it come loose? Finally, I pried it out. Just then, something moved behind my reflection. Oh, no! Right behind the glass, a boy my age was smiling! Had he seen the whole ugly operation? Too embarrassing! I turned and ran. It was definitely time to get to school.

Abigail Adams Junior High School looked like it had been built twice—once about a hundred years ago, and then later, when someone tried to make a modern fashion statement on both ends. The old, yellow brick middle part had stone steps, double front doors, lanterns, a steep roof, and a clock tower that belonged in a postcard of "Scenic New England," just like the trees on Corey Hill. But the two long sides pointing toward the street were just big, ugly, yellow brick rectangles. Right in front of the school was a little old house with a picket fence that looked like it had been plunked down in the schoolyard by mistake.

Trying to blend in, I followed a group of giggling girls toward the rectangle on the right. They looked so old. Two other girls cut in front of me, shrieking and hugging, "OMIGOD! I HAVE THOSE SHOES TOO!" I wondered which door I was supposed to go in.

"Excuse me," one of the giants said, "You must be lost." She pointed to a sign: Eighth Grade Entrance.

"Sorry," I mumbled. "Do you know where the seventh-grade entrance is?"

"I don't really remember. That was *such* a long time ago." They all laughed. "Just ignore them," said another. "Seventh-grade orientation is over there." She pointed to the little house. I turned and hurried toward it. I was already late. I rattled the gate in the picket fence, but the stupid thing wouldn't open. Odd ... Why was I the only one here?

When I looked back at the eighth graders, they were laughing hysterically—at me. I should have guessed that it was a complete setup.

I heard a gentle voice behind me.

"Good morning. You look as if you could use some help."

A tall, elegant, silver-haired woman took my arm.

"Isn't this a wonderful house?" she asked. "The founder of Brookline grew up in this house, and the city moved it years ago to preserve it. But I have a feeling this isn't quite where you want to be. Are you looking for the seventh-grade entrance?"

I nodded.

"Come with me. We'll go right up the center stairs of the middle building. The seventh-grade hall is just inside."

As I looked toward the building, a bell rang and the last of the kids dashed inside.

"Who's your homeroom teacher?" asked the woman.

I pulled out my letter and showed it to her.

"Oh, Ms. Rodriguez," she read, smiling. "'My granddaughter's in that class, too. Go through the big double doors and turn left. Then go all the way to the end of the hall. Room 124 is the last classroom on the left."

"Thank you so much," I said, already running toward the steps. What a nice grandmother. I wished I had a grandmother like that to drop me off at school.

The long hall was lined with lockers and nearly empty. I could hear first-day welcomes through the doors of the classrooms I sped past. I was late, but except for a red-haired girl brushing her hair, at least I didn't have to dodge anyone.

I don't dodge well. In Australia, they put me on defense. I was a good stopper. What's bad in the hallway can be good on the soccer field.

And suddenly, I was there: Room 124. Was I late on the first day? I stood there for a second to make sure I wasn't gasping for air. "Stay calm," I thought to myself. "You can break the cycle of first-day disasters. Just take a breath." I straightened my glasses, squared my shoulders, and got ready to make my entrance.

HOW TO MAKE AN ENTRANCE

I opened the heavy wooden door—which creaked loudly—and tried to sneak in as well as you can when an entire class is looking at you. My bag caught on the doorknob, and I was yanked backwards. Some kids giggled, and a short girl in the front row even laughed out loud.

All I wanted to do was get to my seat. All the desks were in four neat rows. Unfortunately, only two were still empty ... both dead center.

"Welcome," said the teacher, walking over.

So much for sneaking to my seat!

"I'm Ms. Rodriguez."

She reached out her hand. My palms were sweaty as I shook her hand.

"I'm Charlotte Ramsey," I mumbled and slunk down the row toward an empty desk.

I sat down as fast as I could. The girl sitting next to me looked more like seventeen than thirteen. I couldn't help gulping as I sneaked a look at her tight, low-cut jeans and her T-shirt, which showed about three inches of skin every time she moved. Lip gloss, mascara, perfectly streaked hair ... she made me feel like I was dressed for fourth grade, not junior high. The blonde girl behind her, who looked like a clone with the same tank top and jeans, coughed meaningfully and flicked her hair. They both sneaked a look at me, caught each other's eyes, and smirked. They may as well have just said it out loud: "*Loser.*" Oh well. Now I knew who to avoid at lunch—Mascara Girl and Co.

Suddenly, the door swung open and we all turned to look at ... an empty doorway. Just when it was getting spooky, in strolled the red-haired girl I had seen brushing her hair in the hall. She had a laptop case slung over shoulder. I admired her confidence. She didn't seem to have a care in the world.

"And you," said Ms. Rodriguez, "must be Maeve."

"Yes," said Maeve, as she tossed back her hair. "I'm Maeve Kaplan-Taylor." She struck a pose that showed off her figure. Were there hormones in the drinking water here? Would it happen to me?

"Good morning, Maeve," continued Ms. Rodriguez, "that desk is for you."

"Thank you, Ms. Rodriguez. I'm so pleased to be here."

"Just have a seat," said Ms. Rodriguez in a way that wasn't mean, but you wouldn't want to mess with.

Maeve worked her way back to the empty desk in front of me like a character in a musical, right before they start singing—sorta swoopy with pauses on her cork-soled platforms. She sat and arranged her hair again, turning to check out the boys around her. "Wow," I thought, "quite an act." But unlike Mascara Girl next to me, Maeve seemed to be having fun all on her own. I want to find out more about Maeve. But not right now. Ms. Rodriguez was standing at the front of the class, waiting for our attention.

THE "LUNCH" ASSIGNMENT

Our teacher was gorgeous; her shiny black hair, which she held back with a silver clip, hung almost to her waist. Her tan skin made her perfect white teeth stand out when she smiled. She wore a turquoise silk top and silver earrings and a matching necklace. Her black pants swished and her heels clicked as she strolled through the room. She looked smart.

"Welcome to Abigail Adams Junior High," she said. "You come from eight different elementary schools and many different neighborhoods. One of you even lived on a houseboat in Paris last year!"

Everyone looked around to try to figure out who the resident alien was. I pretended to look around, too. I really didn't want to stick out. Out of the corner of my eye, I thought I caught Ms. Rodriguez smiling. The boy on my left introduced himself as Robert. He looked harmless, if a bit nerdy. Past him was another boy who looked familiar, but that didn't make sense. I didn't know anyone.

Ms. Rodriguez went on, "The seventh-grade team and I worked hard this summer to blend the elementary school groups. Most of you will know at least one other person in this homeroom."

At that point, everyone except me seemed to grin or give a thumbs-up to someone. Then it hit me. The boy past Robert was the face behind the bakery window. He had long eyelashes and dark brown eyes that sparkled as he looked right at me. Yikes! Look away. Look anywhere else!

Ms. Rodriguez, catching my eye, said, "Even if you don't

know anyone, by midwinter break you will know the twenty-three other people in this room. And if I've done my homework as well as I *think* I have, some of you will turn out to be close friends."

I sure hoped she was right. After a move, I could usually hold onto a best friend until maybe March. The rest would be gone within months. It's always the same—a June goodbye party with lots of hugs and promises to visit and never forget. Then constant emails over the summer. Then, week by week, it gets harder. The old friendship fades into the new school year until there is nothing left to talk about. So you just stop talking. The friends I made in Paris would be gone by Christmas, except for Sophie.

Ms. Rodriguez took a breath, probably bracing herself for the reaction she knew she'd get from her next statement.

"I've divided you into lunch groups."

Everyone groaned except me. Actually, that's not true. I groaned too, but I was faking. For once in my life, I wouldn't be humiliated on the first day of school trying to find someone to sit with.

"You'll recognize our class's tables in the cafeteria," Ms. Rodriguez continued. "They're the ones with the red-checked tablecloths and place cards."

Somebody whispered, "An Italian restaurant ... maybe we'll get pizza."

A tall, confident girl with gold hoop earrings raised her hand. "Yes, Katani," said Ms. Rodriguez.

Impressive—she already knew our names.

"Do any other classes have assigned seating?"

"I doubt it, Katani," said Ms. Rodriguez. "But they probably don't have tablecloths either. One of my rules is never to look sideways at what other people are doing but instead, do what I feel is right. I believe in treating you at school the way I'd treat you as guests in my home. This is your first day of seventh grade, and I want it to be special. I've thought carefully about the seating arrangement and your lunch partners. After you've eaten together about eight weeks, you'll have a writing assignment to do about each other. Then, you may move to free seating."

Katani flounced into her chair. She did not look happy.

THE WHISPERERS

The rest of the morning was spent going over class schedules, notebook requirements, and homework guidelines. All three grades at Abigail Adams Junior High get a room for meetings and stuff. The seventh grade room is the smallest, since we're the bottom of the heap. It's really more of an oversized closet, with a couple of blue sagging couches, right across from the first row of lockers. But I got the feeling that not just anybody could hang out on those couches. Those two stuck-up girls from homeroom were holding court there, with a couple of other girls hanging on every word they said.

I found my locker, #117, right away. It was a little squishy getting in there, but great to have my very own locker! I organized my notebooks and books on the top shelf. Maeve, the redhead, was right next to me, and the guy from the bakery was on my left. I tried not to look at him, because I was embarrassed about that morning's "teeth in the window" incident. I just hurried to get done.

"So Nick," said Mascara Girl's friend, "I'm not so sure Avery will make it as a goalie. She's too short."

So that was his name ... Nick.

"What you do in Summer League counts less than fall

season, Anna," he answered. "You only got a win off Avery in a sudden death shoot-out. I bet YOU couldn't stop a penalty kick."

"Sticking up for her, huh? Is there something we need to know, Nick?"

"Hey, she's the U-12 premier team goalie. I don't need to stick up for her, Anna," Nick answered with a disgusted look on his face.

I was glad to know that mean, blonde Anna was no friend of Nick's, and I guess not Avery's either. Who was Avery? I went back to class.

CAFETERIA NEGOTIATION 101

When the lunch bell rang, I followed the flow of kids to the cafeteria. It took me a while to figure out the food lines. I'd never been in a cafeteria with so many choices: Deli, Hot, Salad Bar? Not the salad bar. Mascara Girl and Anna were there whispering and pointing at everyone who walked by. I had to admit, they *were* good-looking, or the twin outfit thing would never have worked.

I headed for the hot lunch line and copied the moves of the kids in front of me. "French toast sticks?" yelled a woman wearing plastic gloves. I'd never seen anything close to the funny yellow things she was serving. I must have paused too long, because she snagged the plate on my tray and shoveled a pile of them onto it. Then she dumped sticky brown syrup over them. It was kind of scary, but I didn't know how to escape now.

"Hey, don't forget this!" It was Nick. He handed me silverware wrapped in a napkin.

"Follow me. Our class is way over there."

"Er, thanks," I mumbled.

This was some kind of test, wasn't it? Meet a nice kid in the new school on day one, but before you can even talk to him, you must carry a fully loaded, sticky tray across a crowded room. Wild kids waving, high-fiving, pulling chairs, sticking out feet—so many feet. Please, I prayed, let my first-day-of-school curse be broken. I held the tray tight and charged after Nick. He wove through the tables and kids like a superhero in a video game. I followed as close as I could.

Nick put down his tray at the first of six tables with Ms. Rodriguez's tablecloths and place cards. "You're right there," he said, pointing to the next table.

I made it. I made it in one piece. I passed the test!

"Thank you," I said, with a wave. Syrup from my mystery meal must have gotten on my hand and napkin. All I know is that it looked like I was waving a white flag of surrender. I tried to shake it off. No luck. Nick pretended not to notice, but he was holding back a smile.

◌ଓ

My lunch table was not so polite. The short kid who had laughed at my bag getting stuck on the classroom door knob giggled as I approached. She was getting on my nerves.

Katani, the queen of confidence, rolled her eyes.

Maeve pulled me into my chair. "Welcome, Dorothy," she said loud enough for all to hear.

"Dorothy?" I said. "Who's that?"

"From *The Wizard of Oz*, of course."

Did she think I was from Oz? Did I seem that weird? Then she lowered her voice.

"You're blocking my view of the cutest boy in the school." Maeve nodded toward Nick.

Katani looked at the mess on my plate and shook her

head. In her tiger-striped top, gold chain necklace, and big hoop earrings, she looked like a supermodel. Next to her, I felt like a fashion loser.

I tried to wipe the syrup off my hands. It was like super glue. As I rubbed my napkin to shreds, my bracelets clattered. I caught Katani staring. Had I worn too many? I pulled down my sweatshirt to cover them. Argh! Now my sweatshirt was sticky.

"So ... You are zee one, the special girl from Paris, am I right?" asked Maeve.

"How'd you know?" I asked.

"No one else carries their stuff in a stylin' bag like that," Maeve said. "Besides, you turned ten shades of red when Ms. Rodriguez said 'Houseboat.'"

"Oh," I said, blushing again, wishing I could've been more brilliant than "Oh."

Of course, I didn't realize everyone here carried backpacks. Just another sign I was not fitting in. Oh well, at least she liked my French flea market bag.

The small girl inhaled a yogurt she must have brought from home, and then began waving frantically at Ms. Rodriguez, who dashed to our table.

"When do we go out for recess?" asked the girl.

"My heavens, Avery! Is that all you need? I thought someone was choking! There is no recess in junior high."

Avery scowled.

"Don't worry, you'll have gym twice a week," said Ms. Rodriguez with a smile as she turned away.

"That stinks," said Avery. She slumped in her chair and shot a rubber band off her braces.

"Hey—anyone see *American Idol* last night?" asked Maeve.

"Oh I did," chimed in Katani. "What's up with that

blonde singer's dress?"

Smile. Pretend to look interested even though you have no idea what they're talking about. I peeked at my hands under the table, scraping the last bit of napkin off my fingernails.

That's when I saw my zipper was open. Wide open. What underwear did I have on? Please not the ones with the days of the week from Aunt Alice. That would be even worse than the purple pig underwear incident in Port Douglas. If I had flashed the entire seventh grade now, Avery would definitely be laughing. My sweatshirt must have covered my fly. Whew!

"Don't look down," I thought. "Just act as if nothing horrible happened."

Slo-o-o-o-wly, I found my zipper and ever so carefully, zipped up my pants. Fine. Everything was going to be fine. Inhale. Exhale. Just fine.

"Who do you want to win, Charlotte?" Maeve asked.

"Huh?" I said.

"You know ... *American Idol*?"

If there's one topic I dread, it's American movies, music, and television. Even though I've visited my cousins in Columbus every summer, I am always behind. So, I never know what they're talking about. There's always a new movie or rap star or strange TV game show, and I'm forever struggling to catch up. With a whole year ahead of me, there might be hope, but right now, all I wanted to do was change the subject. Luckily, the bell rang.

"I don't want to be late twice in one day," I said, jumping up as fast as I could.

As I hurried from the table, so did the tablecloth. In that moment it seemed as if time had stopped. Looking over my shoulder, I saw Avery ducking, Katani backing away, and Maeve not yet getting it. In the air between us hung a terrible, awesome constellation of trays, French toast sticks, dishes, salad, place cards, cups, cartons, milk, and utensils.

The moment faded, and then, everything came crashing down before me.

"Eeeeew!!!" screamed Katani as a milk carton flew into her lap and syrup splattered her top.

"Coooooool, yeah!" clapped Avery, swatting back a bowl, as trays and utensils smashed to the floor.

There was dead silence as all eyes in the cafeteria turned toward ... me.

What happened? And why were they all staring down at my pants?

I looked down to see my worst fear come to life. I, Charlotte Ramsey, without help, on the first day of school, in front of an absolutely full cafeteria, had zipped a tablecloth into my pants, and yanked four trays' worth of food, syrup, and milk to the floor.

The cafeteria erupted in cheers. A table of boys held up score cards they drew on napkins: 10, 10, 10, 10. They were right—it was the perfect disaster. Maybe my best ever.

I wrestled with my zipper to release the stupid tablecloth. By that time, my fingers were so sticky I couldn't unzip my pants. I'd done it again. The "First-Day-Disaster Curse" had struck again. All I could do, with 640 eyeballs staring at me, was throw the tablecloth over my shoulder like a Roman toga, and head to the nearest exit. I made it through the applause, laughter, hoots, and a sea of grinning faces, and pushed open the door.

CR

Out in the corridor, I collapsed against the wall. How could something as simple as lunch go so wrong?

Someone said, "It's just the first day. It gets easier. How can I help you?"

It was the tall, friendly grandmother-type who had rescued me that morning. Was she my guardian angel?

"Can you put me on the next plane to Paris?" I asked.

"Do you think that would fix everything?" she asked, a smile barely showing.

I shook my head and tried to blink back tears.

"We haven't formally met," she said, shaking my sticky hand. "I'm Mrs. Fields, and if I remember correctly, the name on your paperwork this morning was Charlotte."

"Charlotte Ramsey," I mumbled.

"Well, Charlotte Ramsey, come with me."

With that, she picked up the end of the tablecloth and walked down the hall beside me, chatting cheerily, as if it were the most normal thing in the world for her to be holding the end of my red-checked toga.

We finally made it to the front of the school, where Mrs. Fields opened the door to the main office. She led me behind the tall, gray counter, past two office ladies at their desks. One of them handed her a stack of pink memos as we walked by. The other peered over her glasses and smiled at me.

"Meet my friend, Charlotte Ramsey," Mrs. Fields said to her. "Charlotte, this is Ms. Sahni. If you ever need to know anything, ask her. She's the power behind this school."

"Nice to meet you Charlotte," said Ms. Sahni. "That's an interesting wrap you have."

I blushed again.

"Don't worry, Charlotte," said Ms. Sahni. "It will get better. It always does."

I sighed heavily. First day, I thought, first day.

"Can you still cover for me this afternoon?" Mrs. Fields asked Ms. Sahni. "I wouldn't want to disappoint the girls."

"Don't I always?" she answered. "Just don't forget my rate's gone up. I want two pieces of the famous apple crisp this year."

"It's a deal," said Mrs. Fields as she opened the door marked "Principal."

Wow. I was certainly getting around, today. Oh well, maybe it wasn't so bad having the school principal for a guardian angel.

"Please sit down," Mrs. Fields said, dropping the tablecloth and pointing to a chair. "Just give me a minute, and we'll get you sorted out."

Quotes, written in beautiful gold cursive on black paper, lined the wall behind her desk. I read them as Mrs. Fields skimmed her messages.

I have a dream that my four little children will one day live in a nation where they will not be judged by the color of their skin but by the content of their character.
—Martin Luther King

Underneath it was:

Ask not what your country can do for you—ask what you can do for your country.
—John Fitzgerald Kennedy

A bird doesn't sing because it has an answer. It sings because it has a song.
—Maya Angelou

I smiled when I saw a quote that survived all my moves:

You must do something to make the world more beautiful.
                                        —Miss Rumphius

I guess I hadn't smiled in a while, because Mrs. Fields noticed the change.

"Recognize something?" she asked.

"Yes. *Miss Rumphius* was one of my favorite books when I was little."

"It's one of my favorites now that I'm a grownup," said Mrs. Fields. "I love the idea of one person making a difference simply by making her own neighborhood a more beautiful place to live, don't you?"

I nodded—she was right—but the main reason I loved the book was that I remembered my mother reading it to me. Sometimes when I read *Miss Rumphius* or *Charlotte's Web*, I close my eyes and can still hear her soft voice and smell her perfume. I wish she were here, now.

Mrs. Fields opened the bottom drawer of a large metal cabinet. A hammer, a saw, a wrench, a long black flashlight, and a shiny pair of pliers lay neatly arranged inside. She picked up the pliers and a spray bottle full of WD-40 and walked toward me.

"Don't worry," she said, spraying on the clean edge of the tablecloth. "When you get to the bathroom, just rub this on the zipper to loosen it up. It will be good as new."

She leaned out the door. "Rita, I'm sending Charlotte out. Could you show her the emergency clothes box and steer her to the office bathroom?"

Ms. Sahni had a whole box of sweatpants and sweatshirts in a closet.

"You're the first this year," she said in a happy voice, as if this were some kind of honor. "Someone had to be. Think how much better you've made everyone else feel who will follow after you."

I appreciated her trying to make me feel better, but it wasn't very comforting to know that I had eased the way for all future school disasters. Any kid who had an accident now would be saying, "At least I wasn't as pathetic as the girl who zipped the tablecloth into her pants."

Even though the office bathroom had concrete walls, it didn't feel much like a school bathroom. There was a rug and a picture of a sailboat with two small children waving. Fresh roses and a basket piled high with cakes of almond soap were on a stand by the sink.

I looked at myself in the mirror. Yuck.

I washed the milk spots off my glasses and picked food from my braids. I didn't even get the worst of it. I'd left that for my lunch partners. Horrible. They'd probably never speak to me again.

After rubbing the zipper with WD-40, it opened enough for me to wiggle out, but the tablecloth was still stuck in the bottom half of the zipper. I pulled on the red sweatpants Ms. Sahni had given me and went back to the office.

Mrs. Fields attacked the zipper with pliers. It didn't seem to fit that this fancy lady in a tailored, cream-colored suit was so handy with a pair of pliers, but she got the tablecloth out in a flash. I wondered how old she was. She had silvery hair but no wrinkles except for the smile lines around her eyes. She must have been even more beautiful when she was young.

✿

Mrs. Fields dropped my pants into a clean garbage bag and handed them to me.

"There you go," she said. "Good as new, minus one round in the washing machine. Now, before you go back to class, tell me a little about yourself. All I know is that you're a seventh grader. Where's home?"

An easy question. But at that moment, it seemed totally complicated. I sure didn't feel like home was Brookline, where I was already the laughingstock of the school. Except for the balcony off my bedroom, nothing about the second floor we rented in the big, old yellow house felt like home yet. Maybe we could move back to Paris before Dad settled into his teaching job. Then I remembered the awful family with the three yelling, runny-nosed little boys who had come to buy our houseboat. They had terrorized Orangina. That was the day she ran away, the last time I saw her ... Next thing I knew I was crying.

"Please don't make me go back to the classroom," I sobbed. "My lunch group hates me."

"Nobody hates you," she said, handing me a box of Kleenex. "Why don't you tell me what happened."

She hadn't seen the looks on my lunch partners' faces when the food and milk and syrup wrecked their clothes. Or when the whole cafeteria started clapping.

Mrs. Fields's telephone rang.

"Which elementary school did you go to last year?" she asked, ignoring it.

"My dad and I just moved here two weeks ago from Paris," I said, sniffling.

"Really?" she asked. "I've always wanted to go to Paris."

She looked so interested, I talked a little more.

"Before that we lived in Australia," I said.

"My goodness!" said Mrs. Fields.

"And before that, Africa," I said proudly.

"No! Not really!" said Mrs. Fields.

"Really," I said. "Tanzania," which came out all nasal and weird since my nose was so stuffed up.

"What an exciting life! You'll have to tell me all about your adventures. I've never been further than Washington, D.C., myself."

"Really?" I asked.

"Really," said Mrs. Fields. "I live in the same house I grew up in, right here in Brookline. Can you imagine that?"

I sure couldn't.

"Ruby," called Ms. Sahni, "I think you're going to need to take this call."

My blotchy face must have looked so pathetic that Mrs. Fields said, "Tell you what, Charlotte. Why don't you help Ms. Sahni stuff envelopes for Parents' Night? Have her clear it with your teacher."

"Thank you, Mrs. Fields," I said, standing up and dabbing my eyes with Kleenex. She paused for a moment. "Would you like to join my granddaughters and me for apple crisp baking this afternoon? It's our annual First-Day-of-School tradition. We'd love to have you."

"Really?" I asked.

"Absolutely. We'd love to have you, Charlotte," nodded Mrs. Fields.

CHAPTER 3

Katani

HOME INVASION

THANKS TO THAT Charlotte girl's performance in the cafeteria, the Pucci knockoff I designed and worked on all of August was history. It was NOT cheap—that silk fabric cost me two weeks of babysitting.

I was in the bathroom trying to clean up when Maeve, the red-haired flirt with the laptop and designer jeans, walked in.

"Do you believe that girl?" she whined. "I look like I just went through a car wash! Do you have any idea how bad milk smells after five minutes?"

Whatever. She hadn't sewn everything she was wearing. Rich kid.

The bell rang.

"Come on, Katani!" she said. "We're gonna be late."

Like I actually cared. I worked on the spots for ten minutes, did the best I could, and walked back into the classroom slow and easy. That's my thing. Never let them see you sweat. Attitude is everything.

"Katani," said Ms. Rodriguez.

"Yes," I said, not looking up in any hurry, expecting to

get yelled at. But Ms. Rodriguez surprised me.

"We're writing down our first impressions of our lunch partners in the blue journals I've passed out. What you write is for your eyes only. I won't be collecting them."

What's up with that? I thought. What teacher gives an assignment and then doesn't read it? I wasn't buying it. Ms. Rodriguez had to be watched.

Katani Summers—First Impressions

Since you're not reading this, Ms. R (ha ha) here's your fashion report card:

Hair: A-
Nice shine, no split ends, natural color. Lose the clip.

Nails: B as in Boring
Nice shape but clear nail polish? What's the point?

Clothes: C as in classic teacher
A little too serious if you ask me.

Jewelry: A-
Like the bold statement. Big earrings, big necklace, lots of rings. But turquoise and silver is last year. Try to go mod.

Accessories: F
No belt? No scarf? Que pasa?

Attitude: A
Love the way you walk in high heels. Must try that.

Maeve's Fashion Report Card:

Hair: A-
Beautiful, natural red. Wish I could bottle that color. Smells like Herbal Essence, though. Way overstyled. Lose the gel and stop straightening. Free your natural, luxurious wave!

Nails: W as in WOW!
Are they for real? I want that color.
Smile: A as in amazing
How do you get dimples like that?
Clothes: L for label hound and E for expensive.
Do your parents buy you anything you want? Is that why you're using a $1,500 laptop in the seventh grade instead of writing with a free pencil like everyone else? BTW ... what's with the shirt? We're not on MTV.
Jewelry: C for cool
Saw those earrings at the mall but couldn't afford them. Cool rings.
Attitude: F for Flirt.
Why do you keep smiling at the guy at the next lunch table? Isn't our conversation interesting enough? Don't you have anything to think about besides boys? Time to get a real life, sister.
Presentation: O for Out there.
What's with the big words and dramatic poses? Who says stuff like "I absolutely adore him"?

Avery's Fashion Report Card:

Hair: S for Same old, Sporty. Soccer pony tail.
Nails: F
Does the word nailbrush mean anything to you?
Smile: C-
Giggle overload. Quit playing with the rubber bands on your braces.
Clothes: D
How many team logos must we wear at once?
Jewelry: F

Hello?
Accessories: F
A yo-yo is not an accessory.
Attitude: C-
Sporty, sporty, and did I say sporty? Probably a sports snob who will laugh at me in gym when she finds out I stink at basketball even though I'm really tall.

Charlotte's Fashion Report Card
Hair: C
Loosen up. Undo the braids. Let your hair down.
Nails: D as in Disaster
Smile: C-
Clothes: C
What are you hiding? Come out from under that hoody.
Jewelry: A+
Super fantastic bracelets. I want.
Accessories: F
Hello? Bonjour?? You lived in Paris. You must have a bunch of them. Where are all your scarves and belts?
Attitude: D-
Ouch. Get this girl some klutz insurance. She's a total spaz.

I closed my journal. "How do we know she won't just look at them after we leave?" I thought.

Just then, like she had psychic powers, Ms. Rodriguez said, "You'll just have to trust me, Katani."

Was that freaky or what? It felt like her eyes were

penetrating my brain. When the bell rang, I bolted for the door—forget the rules. I just wanted to get away from that stare and ride home in my grandmother's car. Grandma Ruby is the principal of our school. Everyone in Brookline loves her, so when you're riding in the front seat beside her, you feel like a celebrity. All the years of elementary school, I had watched my older sisters pull into the driveway laughing and chatting about school in Grandma's car, the Triple B (Big, Blue, Buick). Finally, it was my turn! No more walking home!

Being the youngest is a pain. I'm the last to do everything. Candice, my oldest sister—18, brilliant, gorgeous—says I have it easy. Candice has no idea what she's talking about. For one thing, she never did anything wrong. Her worst tragedy was getting one B+ last year. All she did was set a standard none of the rest of us could live up to.

Patrice, my second oldest sister—16, sports superstar, beautiful—says I'm spoiled rotten. She thinks I whine to get what I want. Personally, I believe Patrice is the bossiest older sister on the planet. I'm glad she's at the high school this year. The only thing is, now I have to pick up Kelley.

Kelley, who is two years older than I am, has a kind of autism. That means she does stuff like carries a teddy bear, talks too loud, and imitates cartoon characters even though she's fourteen and almost six feet tall. Also, she can't handle noise. We can't even go to restaurants or stores that play music, or she starts groaning and covering her ears.

I love her anyway, because she's always happy and happens to be the most truthful person I know. She says the first thing that comes into her mind—what everyone else is thinking but doesn't dare say out loud, which can be really funny. Like in elementary school, our principal wore a hairpiece that seriously looked like road kill. Whenever he walked by, Kelley would say, "Good morning, Mr. Plenning. Why are you wearing a squirrel on your head?"

Sometimes it's easier to love Kelley at home, away from the stares, the whispering, and the jokes. I hate the kids who make fun of her and I hate myself for feeling embarrassed in front of them. If they tried their whole lives, they could never be as nice or as happy as Kelley is. So, why should I care what they think? I know I shouldn't, but I do ...

"Hi Katani! Hi Katani!" Kelley yelled. Ms. Mathers—her aide—had a hard time keeping her from running right at me. A group of kids walking down the hall moved away. They always do that when I'm with Kelley, like she's contagious or something. It's so ignorant. But still, I rushed her through the hall.

"Hi Kelley—ooof!"

Her hug almost knocked me flat.

"You look stunning, Katani!"

Kelley uses words she memorizes from TV commercials.

"Thanks, Kelley. Say thank you to Ms. Mathers."

"Thank you Ms. Mathers," said Kelley. "Have a scrumptious day, Ms. Mathers!"

Ms. Mathers laughed and gave me a wink. "Thank you, Kelley, I'll do that." I steered Kelley to the right.

"Hey, what's that on your CHEST, Katani?" she said, noticing the stains.

She always knows exactly what I'm worried about. All the kids in the eighth-grade hall turned to look. How embarrassing! I grabbed her arm and walked as fast as I could.

All of a sudden, a bell rang right over our heads. Kelley dropped her bear and covered her ears with both hands. "Keep going, Kelley," I urged. A crowd of kids rushed past, trampling her stuffed animal.

Once the bell stopped ringing and she could uncover her ears, she shouted, "I've lost Mr. Bear!" she cried. "IT'S A TRAGEDY!"

The tank-top twins from my homeroom were whispering to some guys with muscles and football jerseys and pointing. Figured those two had already discovered the eighth-grade boys and needed someone to make fun of to get attention. I gave them a "Get a life" glare. Where was that stupid bear?

Kelley kept yelling, "IT'S A TRAGEDY!" as packs of kids rushed at us.

"Please don't melt down, Kelley," I prayed.

Her tantrums are not pretty. She can wail like a siren. Once she gets started, there's no stopping her. Kelley looked ready to lose it. Help!

Just as I reached to pick up Mr. Bear, a girl accidentally kicked him across the corridor. At least she apologized. I raced to capture him, then held the bear in the air so Kelley could see. She beamed.

"TOUCHDOWN, KATANI!" she yelled.

The muscle beach football players yelled "Whoooah!"

"Come on, Kelley," I said, handing her the bear. I put my arm in hers, strolling down the hall as cool as I could. I couldn't wait to get home!

When we turned the corner, Grandma was waving to us from the end of the hall. All I wanted to do was sit next to her in the Triple B and pour out my whole crazy day. She'd be able to figure out how to get the spots out of my new top and make everything right. Grandma Ruby can figure out anything.

"I'll be right along, sweetheart," she called. "Come on in and say hi to Ms. Sahni while I get my briefcase organized. Everyone ready to make apple crisp?"

I *love* Grandma's First-Day-of-School apple crisp. So does

Kelley. She galloped ahead of me and shoved open the door. "Hello, Ms. Sahni!" I heard her shout. "You look ravishing today, Ms. Sahni."

Someone laughed and I knew it wasn't Ms. Sahni. It was a kid's laugh. Who was laughing at Kelley this time? All I wanted to do was get home.

HERE WE GO AGAIN ...

I opened the office door and saw ... the walking cafeteria catastrophe! So this is where she'd been all afternoon. Grandma must have felt sorry for her. Her eyes were red and puffy and matched the bright, red sweats she was wearing. She was sitting in a chair next to Ms. Sahni.

Grandma appeared out of her office. "Girls, I'd like you to meet my new friend, Charlotte Ramsey."

I grunted a "hi" and turned toward the door. Time to get going. I couldn't wait to tell Grandma Ruby that that was the girl who had ruined my day.

"Hello, Charlotte Ramsey!" chirped Kelley. "Are you our new best friend?"

Boy, Kelley can be embarrassing. I wished Grandma would hurry up.

"Katani," said Grandma. "You may have met Charlotte already. You two are in the same homeroom."

Met her! I'd already been slimed by her!

"Er, Katani and I are in the same lunch group," an embarrassed Charlotte mumbled.

Grandma looked me right in the eye, "Well. Isn't it nice you two know each other already. I've invited Charlotte to come home with us and bake apple crisp this afternoon."

Say, what? This girl had wrecked my lunch, my silk top, and now ... my afternoon? I don't think so.

But Grandma didn't seem to get it.

"Come on, girls," she said. "Apple crisp time!"

"Happy Birthday!" shouted Kelley. "Apple crisp time!"
Kelley led the way to the parking lot as if she were marching
in a parade, swinging her arms, and singing, "Happy
Birthday to you. Happy Birthday to you. Happy Bi-i-i-rthday
Apple Crisp! Happy Birthday to you."

I couldn't even look at Charlotte. She was probably
laughing at my sister. I hated her. Not just for that—but for
barging in on my family. When we got to the Triple B,
Grandma offered the front seat, my seat, to "our guest." I
threw myself down on the back seat next to Kelley and
slammed the door.

"How was your first day, Katani?" asked my grandmother.

"OK," I mumbled.

"What did you do?"

"I dunno."

"Did you like Ms. Rodriguez?"

"She's OK." I wasn't going to talk. I was going to punish
Grandma. If she wanted conversation, she'd have to talk to
her new friend, the rat sitting in my seat. "Charlotte tells me
she lived on a houseboat in Paris all last year and Australia
and Africa before that. Her father writes books."

"Show off," I thought. "Why don't you just move back
to Parisaustraliaafrica?" I was silent for the rest of the ride.

At home, Grandma asked me to give Charlotte a tour of
the house while she got the ingredients ready. Why would
this girl care about a two-family house? She'd lived all over
the world. She'd probably lived in palaces. All I had to do
was stand in the kitchen and point. Some tour.

Grandma invited Charlotte to sit on *my* special stool, the
one I always pull up to watch her bake. "Katani, honey, get

some chairs for you and Kelley, would you?"

"Fine," I said in my grouchiest voice. Could it possibly get any worse?

"I'm hooooome!"

Yes, it could.

"Hello, Patrice. How was your day?" asked my grandmother, giving her a hug.

"Soooo much better than junior high," she said. "They give us so much more independence!"

I swear Patrice says things like that just to annoy me.

"Meet our new best friend Charlotte Ramsey!" announced Kelley.

"Hi Charlotte. I'm Patrice."

Charlotte had the same awestruck look on her face all my friends do when they first meet Patrice or Candice. Like they're the coolest things on earth. At least Candice was away at college.

The better Charlotte got along with Patrice, Kelley, and my grandmother, the madder it made me. By the time the apple crisp was ready, everyone was having a fabulous time, and I was ready to stomp off to the bedroom. I would have, too, if I hadn't known Kelley would follow me. That's the trouble with this place. There's nowhere to be alone.

Patrice handed me a bowl and the electric beater. "Katani, since you obviously don't want to talk, why don't you make yourself useful?"

"I am being useful," I answered.

"Yeah, right," she said. "As what, a seat warmer?"

That cracked Kelley up and I caught Charlotte smiling. That did it! I switched the beater on high and pretended they were all in the mixing bowl. Lucky for me Grandma was busy with the next batch of crisp and didn't see my attack on the whipped cream. If she had, she would have given me the "Anything done without love is a waste of time" lecture.

"Where's my whipped cream?" called Grandma, walking over to check the bowl. "Oh dear," she said, clucking her tongue. "I'm afraid you've turned it into butter."

Of course, Patrice had to look and comment, "And you only had one thing to do, too," she said.

"IT'S A TRAGEDY!" yelled Kelley.

"It will be all right," said my grandmother, putting her arm around me. "You'll see. We'll make apple butter."

I tried hard not to cry.

"But Grandma Ruby," Kelley interrupted. "What if our new best friend doesn't like apple butter?"

That's when I completely lost it. "She is not our new best friend, Kelley. We only met her today. We don't even know her. And she managed to ruin the top that I worked on all summer long! This girl has got to go!"

Grandma looked like she was the one I had insulted. I felt mean, and I hated Charlotte Ramsey for making me feel mean. I ran to the bathroom and locked the door.

CHAPTER 4

Charlotte

ICE QUEEN, GIGGLE FIT,
AND ATTENTION HOG

HORRENDOUS DAY EQUALS REALLY BAD NIGHT. I got Truffles down again, put on Mom's old jacket, flopped onto my bed, and pulled the comforter over my head.

I cried for the friends I had left behind in France, especially Sophie. I cried for my lost cat, Orangina. Most of all, I cried because the place I hoped would be better than anywhere else in the world had turned out to be worse ... much worse. The First-Day-Disaster Curse was unbreakable. When only hoarse, little gulps came out, I felt a hand on my shoulder.

I will always be grateful Dad didn't ask lots of questions. He sat next to me, patiently waiting until I could talk.

"I've wrecked everything," I sniffed.

"Tell me all about it," he said, patting my head.

I buried my face in the pillow.

"Things don't seem so bad when you share them with someone else."

I took a deep breath and slowly poured out the story of another first-day disaster. This one, the worst. Dad nodded in all the right places.

"No one's going to like me now," I sobbed. "I'll always be known as the spaz with the tablecloth caught in her pants. I wish Sophie was here. I wish Orangina hadn't run away. I wish I could start all over.

"Dad?"

"Yes, honey."

"Do you think I could get another cat in a few weeks, if Sophie doesn't find Orangina?"

"I'm sorry, Charlotte, but you know, no pets. To tell you the truth, I didn't know what we were going to do with Orangina anyway. I was about to call your cousins to take her."

"No wonder she ran away," I said.

"Oh, come on, your cousins aren't *that* bad," Dad said, pulling one of my braids.

"Easy for you to say. You never spent three weeks with Alana, 'the human pin cushion,' asking you which part of her body she should pierce next."

Dad laughed.

"Glad to see you've got your sense of humor back. Since you didn't get much lunch," he said, "how about us whipping up a couple Croque Monsieurs; those were your and Sophie's favorite sandwiches, right?"

"Croque Monsieurs," I said, wiping my eyes.

"Perfect," said Dad. "We'll have a picnic on your balcony."

UNDER THE STARS ...

Dinner with Dad, watching the full moon rise over the city, helped me forget my troubles. As the stars appeared, he taught me a new constellation, the Seven Sisters. "Seven bright stars, all born about the same time, traveling the universe together."

Wish I were one of them, I thought.

"Any homework yet?" he asked.

"Dad," I answered, "it's day one!"

"Well, just so you don't fall behind."

"Very funny," I said. "Have I ever fallen behind?"

"No, sweetheart," he answered, giving me a hug. "No matter where we've lived, you've always been a great student. Your mother would be proud."

Just before bed I emailed Sophie. I was still dreading tomorrow, but turning my disaster into something that would make Sophie laugh made me feel a lot better.

Dad yawned. "Time for me to turn in. I'm still not used to these early morning hours."

```
To: Sophie
From: Charlotte
Subject: help!


hey sophie! i hate¬ hate¬ hate time
differences. i don't want your away
message. i need to talk. where ARE you?
today i landed in the worst lunch group
ever. one girl is as cold as iced coffee.
another starts trying to get attention as
soon as boys are within twenty feet. the
third goes into giggle fits if you do
something dumb. and i sure did some dumb
things today. most of it's too horrible
to repeat and you wouldn't believe me
anyway. hint ... i ended up in the
principal's office in someone else's
pants. she (Mrs. fields¬ the principal)
```

turned out to be really nice and unscary.
she didn't make me go back to class. ok,
i admit it. i was crying my eyes out.
it's just that when she asked me where
home was, i had no answer. NOWHERE! i
blubbered. that's when she invited me
over after school to make apple crisp
with her granddaughters. sounds fun,
right? guess again. one of her
granddaughters is the ice queen in my
lunch group. think of the nastiest
gargoyle on the roof of notre dame,
multiply by ten, and you've got Katani's
expression when she heard i was coming
over for the afternoon. One nice boy in
my class—Nick. He is interested in
travel. i miss you, sophie.
Hugs, charlotte

P.S. could you go back to the dock one
more time to look for Orangina just in
case?

P.P.S. guess what I made dad for dinner?
our specialty: croque monsieurs!

CHAPTER 5

Charlotte

JOCKS AND WHISPERERS

THE AIR WAS CRISP and the sky over Corey Hill was clear and blue. Sun shone through the leaves as I headed down the sidewalk, but I couldn't have felt worse. How could I face those kids?

When I rounded the corner onto Harvard Street, Yuri called, "Hey! Girl from other country! You look more worried than Yuri. No one is allowed to look worrieder than Yuri."

I couldn't help smiling.

"Come here. I tell you why my day is worse than yours." After polishing an apple on his apron, he handed it to me and raised a thick finger.

"So," he began. "The delivery company, they mess up my order. Why they do this to me? I have no peanut butter and no paper towels to sell today. My day is ruined. Americans cannot live without peanut butter and paper towels. Why is this?"

I didn't know about the paper towels, and I've always wondered about peanut butter myself.

"Beats me," I said. "No one eats it except Americans. I

tried to make my friend in Australia eat some. She took one whiff and told me I was out of my mind."

I thought I caught the tiniest upturn of Yuri's mouth. Was that a smile?

"Why you look so down when you so full of stories?" he asked. "What is big problem?"

"Nothing, I guess."

He threw his hands in the air. "You see. What I tell you? You have no problem. It is Yuri who have all the problems. So go away." He waved me toward school.

I was starting to like this guy. He was like some Russian Oscar the Grouch.

I hurried down the rest of the block without looking into the bakery. I did not want to run into Nick. Just thinking about him catching my tooth-picking and tablecloth acts made me cringe. The schoolyard was full of kids. I stayed as far as I could from the eighth and ninth-graders, running up the middle stone steps and into the building.

There are certain types of kids who pop up in every country I've ever lived in. They're as common as McDonald's or Starbucks. One type are "The Jocks" and the other are "The Whisperers." That morning, I had to get past both groups to make it to our classroom. The Trentini twins, Nick, and of course, Avery were hanging right by my locker. They wore baseball caps and pulled, poked, and jostled each other just like they do everywhere else on the planet. As I bent down, Avery shoved Billy Trentini, and he fell into me. My bag flew off and skidded across the hall, scattering my books everywhere as it went.

"Geesh, Avery!" Billy said, laughing. "You almost knocked us both over."

I hurried to pick up my things, as Avery giggled, and

said "Sorry ... Oh, by the way. That was sooo cool yesterday when you took out our table."

I knew I had to get away from her. Now she was throwing fake punches at Nick, and I really didn't want him backing into me as I scooped things back into my bag. I'd already had enough embarrassing moments in front of him.

The Whisperers were huddled by the classroom door. As much as I hated to walk toward them, I knew I couldn't stay where I was. Whisperers come in all languages, but you don't need to understand what they're saying. They all whisper private "in-jokes," point, and laugh really loud. Their purpose is to make everyone else feel left out. In Brookline, their names were Anna and Joline.

I walked as quickly as I could and hoped for the best. They moved even closer together, whispered, and pointed.

"Hey Joline," asked Anna. "What has four eyes, two braids, and a tablecloth sticking out of its pants?" Joline and two assistant Whisperers screeched with laughter.

There was a rapid clicking of heels as Ms. Rodriguez came to the door of the classroom. "Good morning," she said. "Since you're all here and it's time to get started, why don't you come in." Once we were in our seats, Ms. Rodriguez looked right at Anna and Joline with piercing eyes. "This wasn't in the lesson plan but I've had a great idea. Let's spend some time writing in your journals. The assignment is 'My Most Embarrassing Moment.' Let me know if the assignment isn't clear and I'll call on a couple of people to come to the front of the room and share examples."

Joline shifted in her seat.

"Busted," said Nick in a low voice.

"Oh, man," griped Robert. "Bigmouth Anna strikes again and we all end up paying for it."

CHAPTER 6

Avery

TAKE ONE

JUNIOR HIGH STUNK BIG TIME—another journal assignment today. No snacks. No recess. Too much work. And bo-ring, except for the major crash at my lunch table.

Total yard sale! Charlotte, the girl in my lunch group, was awesome. If yesterday was a sneak preview, I couldn't wait to see what she'd do next.

My other lunch partners, Katani and Maeve, are too girly. And now, thanks to Anna and her loser friend, Joline, we have to write another lousy journal assignment.

I turned around and made a face at Anna. I couldn't believe they were both in my class again this year. I thought the teacher said we were only supposed to know ONE other kid in the homeroom. So how did I get doubly pond-scummed? Yesterday, they wore twin tank tops. Must have taken them all summer to plan that one.

I've played on travel teams against bony, blonde "Anna Banana" since I was seven. The only thing she has over me is her height. If it weren't for that, I'd beat her in everything. Joline is an Anna groupie. They're always on the same sports teams. Joline isn't as good as Anna but she makes up for it in nastiness. She's always getting red cards for tripping kids or unnecessary roughness. Beats me how she even sees the ball through all that eye makeup.

When I beat everyone in our school arm wrestling contest last year, she said, "You'll never get the boys to like you that way."

Like I'm supposed to lose to boys to make them like me!

"Avery Madden! It's time to stop wiggling and start writing," said Ms. Rodriguez.

Boy, I hated being in the front row. I decided to reread my first journal entry—First Impressions—before I started today's assignment. I figured it would make me look busy and give me some time to think about what I was going to write next. And I wondered if I had already changed my mind about what I wrote yesterday. I'm like that sometimes.

Avery Madden—First Impressions

Maeve

Why does she keep smiling at Nick? I'm positive he doesn't know her. She wasn't in our school or on any of our teams last year. Too girly-girl. She walks like she's putting on a show and talks like the weird people my mother goes to the opera with. Why does she get to use a computer and the rest of us have to write in these crummy blue notebooks?

Katani

I stink at names, but I know she's Patrice Summers's younger sister so she must be an incredible athlete. Patrice is my varsity soccer role model. She coached me for the city championship. (*I did great until the sudden-death shootout*). I remember seeing this girl cheering for her at the high school night games. She's even taller than Patrice. Excellent basketball player? #1 pick for my team.

Charlotte

The new girl—major entertainment. Her cafeteria disaster was awesome—definitely the best thing that's happened so far in Jr. High. Kind of embarrassing for her, though. I bet she's no good at sports.

Ms. Rodriguez walked by my desk and told me that I better start writing or I would run out of time. School is way too much work.

Avery Madden
My Most Embarrassing Moment

I only got embarrassed once. The time Sally Dennehy asked me in front of a whole bunch of kids at a sleepover if I knew where babies came from. "Duh," I said. "I've seen the video of it a hundred times."

"You have?" They all rushed over. "What was it like?"

"No big deal," I said. "The plane landed. Some lady brought me and the other babies out. Everyone hugged and cried. Then we went home."

Those kids laughed me out of town. How was I supposed to know? I was only six and I'm adopted. I thought all babies came from airplanes.

Good, that's done. I looked around and saw that my other lunch partners were still writing. I hope that doesn't mean that we are going to be late for lunch.

Charlotte Ramsey
My Most Embarrassing Moment

Well, before yesterday's lunch, this might have required some thought. But today it doesn't: Soaking my lunch group, getting the tablecloth caught in my zipper and humiliating myself in front of the whole cafeteria plus lunchroom staff is my most embarrassing moment ever. I hope. Another disaster could ruin any chances for any future happiness.

Maeve Kaplan-Taylor
My Most Embarrassing Moment

```
My most embarrassing moment? You are
obviously kidding, Ms. Rodriguez. Every
time I—and no one else in this class has to
use a laptop computer in class—it screams
"learning issues." Some kid always says
some totally snotty thing when I take my
laptop out. I'm really tired of that, and
it makes me feel dumb.
```

Katani Summers
My Most Embarrassing Moment

I still don't believe that this really is a private journal. I will just say that yesterday's lunch was the most embarrassing and trying moment of my life, and that I should be released from the "nightmare" of my assigned lunch group. This is a very sensitive time in our lives. How do you think it felt to have my new clothes splattered with milk, maple syrup, and bits of French toast sticks? How gross! And how about having the entire seventh grade staring at our table? I'll tell you how it felt: HUMILIATING.

CHAPTER 7

Katani

DESPERATE MEASURES

THIS LUNCH SEATING PLAN had to go. I couldn't take another minute with Maeve, the spoiled, rich airhead with the laptop, or Avery, the human jumping bean. And no way was I going to let Charlotte—wrecker of wardrobes, stealer of grandmothers—anywhere near me. I raised my hand.

"Yes, Katani."

"I need to speak with you in private, Ms. Rodriguez."

"Can't it wait 'til lunch?"

"No, I don't think so. This is an emergency."

Ms. Rodriguez motioned me out to the hall. I closed the door and moved away from the window where I could see a curious Avery stretching out of her chair trying to see what was going on.

"What can I do for you?" Ms. Rodriguez asked.

"Ms. Rodriguez, I have a major problem," I said.

"What is it?" she asked, looking concerned.

"I can't possibly eat with my group today."

She raised her eyebrows and glared. "And why would that be, Katani?"

"No offense, Ms. Rodriguez. I know you have a lot on your mind. But you made a mistake putting us together. You want us to learn from each other's differences, but all we're learning is to hate each other. I think you should move us before it's too late."

"Aren't you rushing it a bit, Katani?" she asked. "This is only the second day of school."

"Ms. Rodriguez," I wailed, "yesterday was positively traumatizing for me, and my new top is completely ruined."

I didn't want to tell her about Charlotte coming to our house. It still made me furious. Besides, it was too personal. I didn't like how Ms. Rodriguez already seemed to have me figured out.

She thought for a second. "Katani, I'm very sorry for what happened to you yesterday. I truly am. But how must Charlotte feel? Give it a little time, Katani. We can talk about this tomorrow, if you still feel the need."

"But, Ms. Rodriguez, you have no idea how much damage that girl can do in a day!"

"That's enough, Katani. I want you to give it your best effort today and maybe we can talk about it with the whole lunch group tomorrow."

It wasn't a "Yes." But it wasn't a "No." All I had to do was survive lunch and we could all be done with it tomorrow. Maybe I should wear a raincoat.

CHAPTER 8

Charlotte

SNEAK ATTACK

I STARTED IN THE HOT LUNCH LINE but turned around as soon as I saw what a "Sloppy Joe" was. How could anyone eat chili in a bun? Definitely too high risk for me. I checked out the salad bar area. Whew! No sign of Anna and Joline. Robert, who everyone in the class calls "Mr. Healthfood," was drowning a miniature piece of lettuce in ranch dressing.

"Hi, Charlotte. Don't get too close, this is a clean shirt—just kidding. Boy, yesterday must have been terrible for you."

"I've been through worse," I said, trying to get him to drop the subject.

"Like what?" he asked, really interested. So I changed the subject.

"Why don't you eat something you like?" I asked.

"Mrs. Fields just caught me trying to get ice cream," he grumbled. "My mother had a conference with her in August and told her I'm not allowed to eat anything from school but salad. It's great to be me."

"That's not all you're eating, is it?"

"Nah. I've got two tofu sandwiches on rye, and I paid

Josh a dollar to sneak me a cupcake."

"That sounds good," I said.

"Yeah." He paused. "Oh, and Charlotte ..."

"Yes, Robert."

"Watch your back," he mumbled. "I heard Anna and Joline daring each other to trip you."

"After seeing what I can do all by myself with a tablecloth, you'd think they'd know better. But, thanks for the warning," I said.

"No problem," he said, walking away. "They stuck a 'Kick Me' sign on my blazer in ballroom dancing last year."

I picked up the salad tongs and aimed at a hard-boiled egg. My glasses bonked the plastic hood as I flailed the tongs and knocked the egg off the salad bar. It rolled right under Henry Yurt's shoe. I walked the other way pretending I'd never seen that egg before in my life. I looked over my shoulder in time to catch Henry stepping squarely on the egg, squishing it, and walking on without ever looking down. Henry, who acts really spacey in class, is the only person I know who wouldn't have noticed he'd stepped on an egg.

I was really getting hungry. Maybe a tuna sandwich and soup from the deli line?

I took the longest way possible to our spot. By sticking to the walls, I could avoid passing the tables in the middle of the room. Just Joline's table left to go. And sure enough, she and Anna ducked toward each other, eyes rolling. They both flipped their hair back at the exact same minute and sighed, as if to say, *"What a dork!"* in perfect, nasty harmony. I couldn't help but marvel at them as I tried to wriggle my way through the packed tables. How could they say so much without saying a single thing?

I was tempted to kind of trip and dump the contents of

my tray right on Joline's perfect hair.

When she stuck out her leg, just as Robert predicted, I hopped right over it. Then, I fumbled and pretended to almost drop my tray, which freaked her out and got a laugh from her whole group.

I had tried to keep my soup from sloshing, but spooking Joline had cost me. My sandwich was soaked.

"Pitiful," muttered Katani.

The table was silent without Maeve. Avery stared, waiting for something exciting to happen. Katani wouldn't even look at me. What had I ever done to her? On purpose, I mean.

Finally, Maeve swirled her way over to our table, but she spent most of lunch ogling the boys at the next table— Robert, Josh Trentini, Nick, and a short kid named Sammy Andropovitch—and ignoring the rest of us.

To: Charlotte
From: Sophie
Subject: this and that

ma cherie,
maybe this Nick guy is OK. A friend? ...
tell me more about him. He is the one who saw
you play with your teeth, no? oh charlotte,
you make me laugh always. I am not
laughing so much this year that you are
gone. I laugh only one time today when
our class was helping serve the lunch and
philippe and alain had to wear nets on
their hair. Philippe looked exactly like
his grandmere. I am sorry I never found
orangina. It is too bad you are not

permitted to have pets in your new home.
I cry for you. the girls in your lunch
group sound terrible. But there are trés
difficile girls here, too. Celeste and
Chantal the "whisperers," as you call
them, are always whispering and pointing
comme toujours. I don't like them.
Bisous,
Sophie

CHAPTER 9

Katani

DROPPING THE BALL

THE FIRST GYM CLASS could not have been worse. It was raining, so we had to play basketball inside. When Mr. McCarthy found out I was a Summers, he got a sharky grin on his face and threw me a basketball.

"Show me your moves, Summers," he bellowed.

My first move was to drop the ball.

"I get it." he said. "You're a comedian."

I cleared my throat.

"I'm saving my important moves for the game," I said, trying to act casual.

Mr. McCarthy whistled everyone to center court.

"Summers and Madden will be our captains. Flip for first choice on teams."

He spun a quarter in the air and proudly caught it behind his back like he was a gold medalist in the Coin Tossers Olympics. He only made us captains because he thought I was going to be good, and Avery's skills were famous. I hate it when gym teachers favor the jocks. How are the rest of us ever going to learn to like sports?

I crushed Mr. McCarthy's hopes and dreams in the first five minutes by missing three easy shots and throwing the ball out of bounds. Good. Better to be branded quickly and quietly and get it over with. The only reason my team didn't get completely killed was that once Anna and Joline realized how lousy I was, they hogged the ball and only passed to each other, Nick, and Josh Trentini. Fine with me. See if I care. But I did.

When Avery saw me play, her jaw nearly hit the floor.

When we were changing in the locker room, she asked, "Aren't you Patrice's sister?"

"Yes, Avery," I said, knowing exactly what she was thinking and getting madder by the moment.

"Oh," she said. "You were so bad, I thought you might be adopted."

That did it. "Girl, do you ever think before you open your mouth?" I asked, slamming my locker.

When I stomped out the door, I heard her yell, "Hey! What's wrong with being adopted?"

All I wanted to do was forget about gym class and those awful lunch partners. Maybe a smile from Kelley would help. I took the long way back to our classroom so I could pass the Resource Room. When I turned the corner, I couldn't believe what I saw. Charlotte was standing outside Kelley's door waving. This kid would do anything to get in good with the principal.

"Have a scrumptious day, Charlotte!" hollered Kelley.

I wasn't sure I could make it twenty-four more hours 'til the weekend.

CHAPTER 10

Maeve

THE INVISIBLE GIRL

MAEVE MONTOYA, MRS. MAEVE MONTOYA, Mrs. Nicolas R. Montoya. It had a real movie star ring to it. Just like in *The Princess Bride*. OMG, I love that movie.

Nick Montoya is totally my destiny. And just in case I had a single tiny doubt, I got proof last night at the Golden Pavillion. Listen to what my fortune cookie said: "Watch out ... a special friend is waiting." Could that be any clearer?

And can you believe it? The next day, fate put HIM in my homeroom. How totally romantic is that? We were absolutely meant to be ... as soon as he has a clue who I am. No problem, whatsoever.

After the last bell, I gave Nick a two-minute head start. I didn't want to look like I was stalking him. I even stalled at a few stores on the way, which is no problem, since I absolutely adore shopping. Irving's Toy and Card Shop has every kind of candy you can imagine. My personal favorites are Necco wafers and Swedish Fish. I go there most days after school for a little pick-me-up and a chat with Ethel Weiss. Ethel wears a little badge that says, "I love my customers." She's owned Irving's since forever, which is nearly true since she's almost ninety.

"Hello, Maeve!" called Mrs. Weiss over the crowd of kids at the counter. "Would you like the regular?"

Mrs. Weiss is kind of my surrogate grandma. I try to come in every Tuesday before Hebrew School, and it's not just because I have a complete and total Swedish Fish obsession, either. I like the stuff Mrs. Weiss says. If I've got things on my mind, I can tell her about them.

When I was in second grade, she caught me stealing a Mounds bar. She said she wouldn't tell my parents if I sat down and wrote her a letter of apology right then and there. I struggled for ages. That was before anyone knew I was dyslexic. I spelled almost every word wrong. Totally embarrassing!

"Such beautiful thoughts," she said when I finished. "Never forget what you wrote here, Maeve. You're a very good girl."

Der mrs. Wize,

thank you fer bieng so nice not too tell my parnts abuot the cadny i took. I new it wuz rong but I waz hungree ... I promis nver to steel agen ever. I luv yer stor. It is my favrit. my mom onle give me munny on frida. Sumtime its hard to wate all week to by cadny. But from now on I am watin. Even if my tummy grols and I am drooling I will wate. even if all my frend hav treets besept me, I will wate til I hav munny. Even if I am staving I will wate. frum now on I will lisen to my hart not my tummy. but do not xpec me in yer stor any day but firday. My mom sez I shood save my munny but I can nevr leeve yer stor with out sending all my cash.

Luve and harts,

Maeve Kaplan-Taylor

She saved my letter in the scrapbook she keeps of our whole neighborhood's history. Some day, when I'm a famous actress too old for the glamour roles, I plan to star in the movie of Ethel's life and read from the scrapbook.

Ethel waved me to the counter. "So, how's school?"

"Okay, I guess. We have an absolutely gorgeous teacher. But she gave us some pretty strange homework for tonight."

"Tell me."

"Well," I said, "she wants us to write her a letter about a school rule we'd like to change."

"Sounds creative, just like you. Have fun with it!"

"I'll try, Mrs. Weiss, but you know me and homework."

"What I know is you always give it your best shot."

"Thanks, Mrs. Weiss," I said.

Nick should have had enough of a lead by now.

"Mrs. Weiss, I gotta go."

"Remember, Maeve. Don't sell yourself short. A girl such as you deserves nothing but the best."

"Thanks, Mrs. Weiss."

She waved me out the door.

I backtracked to Montoya's and crossed the street so I could watch Nick without being seen. Through the window, I could see Nick clearing tables. I couldn't stall too much longer. Mom was driving me to one of my five million lessons at four o'clock. My parents are absolutely obsessed with me "reaching my full potential." Sometimes I wish they'd just let me veg on the couch. Was today Suzuki violin or my reading tutor? Whatever.

FINDING AN ACCOMPLICE ...

My biggest worry was how to get the conversation thing going. I needed someone to drag in to the bakery with me.

Luckily, I spotted the girl from my lunch group. She was the klutziest person I've ever met, but I figured that all I needed was a warm body who wouldn't make me look bad. Curled up on the window seat of the bookstore with her nose buried in a book, she looked like the girl in *Princess Diaries*. If she lost the glasses and found some clothes to match the coolness of her bag and bracelets, she actually had potential.

"Hi, Charlotte," I said, snatching her book. She blinked like she was reentering Earth's atmosphere. My brother Sam's the same way when he's reading. Personally, I don't get it.

"Uh. Hi, Maeve."

"Wanna taste the best hot chocolate in the entire world?" She still looked dazed.

"Sure, I guess so."

"Great," I said, putting down her book and grabbing her arm. I pulled her out the door.

"It's not too far, is it?" she asked. "I told my dad I'd stick to Harvard Street, unless I called him."

"No, silly," I assured her, dragging her across the street to the entrance of Montoya's Bakery. "You're going to absolutely LOVE this place," I said.

"Oh, no," she said, stopping cold. "Not here." She looked like she was going to bolt. What was up with her?

I grabbed her arm. "Oh, yes," I answered, and dragged her inside. "Here."

The jingling bell on the screen door announced our entrance. Charlotte was looking a little green. I chattered in her ear while checking the room full of round tables and chairs. No sign of Nick. His older sister, Fabiana, "local legend and star of most of the Brookline High musicals," stood behind a case full of cookies, muffins, and croissants.

"May I help you?" Fabiana asked.

"Two hot chocolates, please."

"I'll bet you both want whipped cream," she said.

Charlotte and I nodded. I absolutely adore this place. Yummy baking smells filled the air: brownies, cakes, and fresh bread. Fabiana squirted mountains of whipped cream into our mugs.

"Chocolate sprinkles on top?" she asked.

We nodded again.

"This place is great," said Charlotte.

"I knew you'd love it," I said. "That's why I brought you in here."

Not really, but with a soup bowl of hot chocolate and Nick in my future, I was feeling warm and fuzzy.

"You look familiar," Fabiana told me.

"Maybe you've seen me in the movies," I said, giggling. "My parents own The Movie House."

"That's it. I've seen you at the candy counter. We've been going to your movie theater since we were little. My father used to drag us to all his old favorites so he could brush up his English. I'm Fabiana."

Like I didn't know her name and every time her family had been in!

"Hi!" I said. "I'm Maeve Kaplan-Taylor and this is my friend, Charlotte Ramsey."

Charlotte smiled. She was looking a little less nervous. I carried our drinks to a window table. Things were going well, but there was no sense in taking any chances.

"Thanks," she said, looking relieved.

Just as we were sitting down, HE came out of the kitchen and glanced at our table. So what if we were the only people in the bakery? It was a meaningful glance. He smiled and walked toward us. As he pulled up a chair, I held my breath.

I wanted to remember his first words forever.

"Did you really live on a houseboat in Paris?" Nick asked.

"I've never been ..." I started to answer.

"Yeah, I did," Charlotte mumbled into her hot chocolate.

Hey! Wait a minute! Who was running this conversation anyway? I better make my move.

"Cool!" said Nick.

"I'm Charlotte's good friend, Maeve," I offered, trying to get things back under control.

"Hi, Maeve" he said, and turned back to Charlotte with a killer smile. "*Nice teeth*," he said, his brown eyes sparkling.

Nice teeth? Was this some code between them? Why was she blushing?

"So," Nick went on, "tell me about the houseboat. I've always wanted to live on the water."

Was I invisible here?

"It wasn't as cool as it sounds," said Charlotte, who had *finally* stopped blushing. "The river was dirty and there wasn't much room. Australia was a lot better."

"Australia?! You lived in Australia? I've always wanted to go diving at the Great Barrier Reef. Have you been there?"

"Sure!" she said. "I lived in Port Douglas. We snorkeled on the reef a lot."

This was annoying. Suddenly, the shy, nerdy bookworm was chatty and smiley. She even looked the teensiest bit pretty! Where did this come from? Help! What could I do?

"I haven't swum in anything but a wading pool since I saw *Jaws*," I joked.

They both gave me blank looks. Hey! Don't you recognize humor when you hear it? On and on, Charlotte droned about going barefoot to school and swimming with sea turtles. Boring, boring, boring. But Nick didn't seem to think so. Hmmpf.

"Wow!" he kept saying over and over, like he was stuck. "Wow!" This was getting too far off my script. Time for a show stopper.

"Hey!" I said. "Wanna see an imitation?"

I stood up and nailed my Janet Jackson moves. Yes! Nick was so obviously enchanted. Then the door jingled and someone rushed in.

"Hey, Nick! You coming?"

Comedy Central ...

I couldn't believe it! Avery, from my lunch group—with a basketball! Was Katani next? If I didn't know better, I'd think THEY were my destiny instead of NICK! All we needed was one of Ms. Rodriguez's checkerboard tablecloths—and that gave me an idea.

"Wait, wait ... One more imitation," I said.

"Cool," said Avery, as Nick and Charlotte agreed. "Great!"

Avery bounced over and sat on the edge of Nick's chair. I hate people who are tiny and cute enough to fit onto other people's destined beloved's chairs. And her constant giggling was distracting Nick. Definitely time for my newest, funniest imitation for him. Something to remember me by the whole time he was away from me.

I grabbed Charlotte's glasses, stuck the tablecloth in my pants, and started to walk away. Laughing, Nick caught our mugs before they hit the floor.

I have to admit—I felt the teensiest bit mean when I saw Charlotte's face, but why'd she have to take it so seriously? It was only a joke.

CHAPTER 11

Charlotte

EMPTY HOUSE

THE WALK UP THE HILL SEEMED TO GO ON FOREVER. It was the same trees and houses, same sidewalk and lamp posts, but my feet dragged like I was walking through mud. I couldn't think of a reason to get home. Even on a good day, 3:30 is an empty time of the afternoon. Right after school is when I miss having my mother the most, which is strange because she died before I even went to kindergarten. It just seems like the time of day someone should be meeting you at the door, greeting you with a snack, and asking about your day. I would have told her how awful it had been ... how each time I thought someone around here was nice, they turned out to be nasty. I know that she would have understood.

I sat on the sidewalk and looked down the hill toward Beacon Street. Some of the houses were as fancy as ours, with turrets and balconies and painted woodwork. I liked our house, but it was empty, and I couldn't figure out a way into the Tower. If I could get into the Tower, I could see past school, past Boston, maybe all the way to the ocean. I was stuck between a lonely house and a school where I was doomed to

❁

be humiliated. Maybe I'd just sit here on the steps—halfway up, halfway down—until winter came and the snow covered me. My face felt hot, and I could tell I was about to start crying ... Was disaster my middle name?

Hey, I said to myself, get a grip, Charlotte. This was only the second day of school ... Dad's right. I've always made friends before. Why would Brookline be any different? I just had to be patient.

I climbed the front porch, and did my usual trick of pretending there's a whole family waiting inside for me. Opening the front door, I ran up the front stairs, and called out, "Hi, everybody! I'm home!"

Then, the strangest thing happened. I heard a voice. At least I thought I heard a voice. I peeked over the banister toward the empty dining room with the dusty chandelier and into the carpetless living room with the grand piano. It must have been an echo in these dusty, old, rooms. All the same, I ran upstairs and turned on all the lights, even though it was still daylight. I headed to my desk, put on my writing jacket, and scribbled Sophie a letter on the barf bag I got from the seat pocket on the flight over.

September 4th

Hey Sophie,

Do you like my barf bag stationery? I snagged it on the plane just for you, mon amie. Speaking of friends, I don't have any here. I thought I did for a few minutes this afternoon. A girl from my lunch group, Maeve, invited me to a bakery. But she ended up completely embarrassing me in front of a bunch of people.

I'm so lonely. There's no one to talk to. Remember Roman Day last year when Monsieur Spurling would only let us talk in Latin? My lunch table is more deathly silent than that. Speaking of lunch, here's one that will make you gag—French toast sticks. Don't worry, there's no translation. Just imagine a piece of sponge left in the sun—although that would have more flavor. I miss those French baguettes so much. Thanks for looking for Orangina. I miss you trés trés trés trés like crazy.
Love,
Charlotte

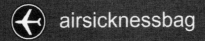
airsicknessbag

CHAPTER 12

Katani

CHANGING THE RULES

MS. RODRIGUEZ HAD GIVEN US the homework assignment
of writing a letter to change something at our school we
didn't like. That wasn't hard. I detested my lunch group.

If I Could Change A School Rule

Dear Ms. Rodriguez,
I don't think it is fair that we have assigned seats at
lunch. First, this is the one time we have to relax with our
friends from other classes. Second, you say we need to
bond with our new classmates, but our bonds with our
old elementary school friends are just as important. Third,
our lunch group really has nothing in common. Fourth, I
design and sew a lot of my own clothes. It would cut into
my homework time if any more of them were ruined by
someone dropping a tray, or trays, or yanking a tablecloth.
I have thought long and hard about the problem and
our chat and about a solution. I think we should have a
sleepover. That way we'll get to know each other quickly

*and then we can move on and sit with other people we like
at lunch time.*

Sincerely,

Katani Summers

I didn't think it was possible, but lunch that Friday was
even quieter than the day before. Something must have
happened between Charlotte and Maeve, because Charlotte
wouldn't even look at her. I wonder what *did* happen? The
sooner this was over, the better for all of us. I was thinking
about Ms. R, and whether she had read my letter, when there
she was, right behind me. She is seriously psychic.

"Girls," she asked. "How is lunch going today?"

We all mumbled "fine" or something like that.

"Well, Katani wrote me an interesting letter last night,"
began Ms. R, "about changing the assigned tables rule.
Thank you for your letter, Katani."

"You're welcome, Ms. Rodriguez," I answered.

The tables near us were listening to every word.

"Katani, it was obvious you thought long and hard about
your assignment. I, too, thought long and hard when I put
the groups together. I appreciate your creativity in suggesting
a sleepover instead of spending the next few weeks getting
to know each other at lunch."

And then she spelled out our chance at freedom.

"With your parents' permission, I'll OK a sleepover this
Saturday. If all goes according to your plan and by Monday
you'd like to move to free seating, I'll honor that. Of course,
you'll still have to fulfill the writing assignment on what you
learned about each other. I'll look forward to hearing how
it goes."

I think the other girls were surprised, but they didn't

look disappointed.

The buzz from other tables started up. I heard Billy Trentini say, "So what if Charlotte spilled some food. Get over it. That Katani is real cold."

"Brrrrrrrr," said a shaking Daniel Jordan. "Where are my hat and mittens?"

That was enough of that.

"Billy," I said, "I just want to sit where I want. They can put me in whatever class they want, but I have a right to be with my friends at lunch."

"What friends, Katani?" asked Henry Yurt.

I thought Avery's milk was going to come out of her nose. Boys can be so stupid. If my name was "Yurt" maybe I'd be stupid, too. I did *not* have time for this.

"Very not funny, Henry. And when was the last party you were invited to?"

Then, I turned and asked, "Who wants out of this ridiculous seating arrangement?"

There was a long, weird pause—one of those pauses when you know everybody's wondering, "Should I do this or not?"

"OK," said Charlotte.

"Me, too," said Maeve, tossing her hair.

"Sure," Avery said between giggles. "Whatever. Charlotte, can I have that napkin?"

"So," I began. "Let's make this as painless as possible. We'll draw for the house, get permission, and meet after dinner Saturday at one of our houses. No reason to drag it out through another dangerous meal."

Charlotte looked away.

CHAPTER 13

Charlotte

LOSING THE LOTTERY

To: Sophie
From: Charlotte
Subject: drama

hey sophie:
it will really be a relief when it's over,
but what happened today still feels weird.
we got our teacher's ok to end the lunch
group if we have a sleepover. we're
supposed to email each other about
permission tonight. katani said "no use
stalling. somebody has to host this thing."
so we drew for it.

the girl who laughs at everything, avery,
put four pieces of paper—three blanks,
one with a big fat S for Sleepover into
her baseball cap. Not me, not me, please
not me i prayed when i pulled out my slip

of paper. i couldn't handle the pressure
of the three witches at my house, even if
they were asleep. at first i thought i
was safe because mine was blank. then I
saw them cheering. the S was on the other
side of my slip. S for Super. just super.
i called dad and got permission, but I
haven't gotten any emails from those
girls yet, so it may not happen. kind of
a no-win situation. wish me luck.

miss you.

charlotte

Chat Room: BSG

File Edit People View Help

flikchic: Cleared it with
the parents. c u tomorrow
@ 7
Kgirl: Me 2
4kicks: ditto
skywriter: ok

4 people here

flikchic
Kgirl
4kicks
skywriter

Dad was way too excited about the sleepover when he got home. I reminded him the girls weren't coming because they liked me, but that didn't stop him from turning into a cleaning tornado. I helped for a while but then I went to my room. I was kind of sad because these would be my first Brookline visitors, my first sleepover, and nobody really wanted to be here. I wasn't even sure I'd show them my room but just in case, I hid Truffles so I wouldn't look babyish. Dad was in his office writing when I went to bed.

"So, we'll get to the store early," he said, "buy a few things for tomorrow night ..."

"Dad," I interrupted, "I think this is getting out of control, don't you?"

But he kept right on talking.

"... and on the way, we'll stop off for pancakes."

"Did you say 'pancakes'?"

He really knows me.

"Thought that would do the trick."

CHAPTER 14

Charlotte

TRUTH AND CONSEQUENCES

I WOKE UP EARLY and, because Dad wouldn't be up for a while, went to check out the park across the street. It wasn't that big, but the lawn seemed to roll away to the edge of the world. I sat on a swing and watched a woman playing with her dog. I'm kind of a cat person ... but that's probably because I've never had a dog.

As I swung up in the air, I could see our house. We had found the place through the housing office at Boston University. I knew why Dad decided to rent the top half of this yellow Victorian with the midnight blue shutters. He loved the possibilities of old homes full of cozy nooks and crannies. I did, too. This one reminded me of a birthday cake, spread with frosting shingles, sugar balconies, and a Tower on top. The wide front steps led up to a grand porch with towering pillars and a porch swing at one corner. Floor to ceiling windows, twice as tall as I was, reflected the golden light of the rising sun on the trees.

When we were looking for places to live, the porch and the balconies were what first captured our attention. The inside of the house was really cool, too. I loved the elegant, winding front stairway leading to the second floor—our floor. The banister was perfect for sliding. I tried it out on our first day in the house.

But it was the windowed room on the roof, the Tower in the center of the house, that sold me. Each of the four sides had a large center window, sandwiched between two smaller windows. It looked like a perfect tower for a writer.

I really wanted to ask our new landlady, Miss Pierce, about the Tower, but we still hadn't seen her yet. The day we signed the lease, the rental agent explained that Miss Pierce lived in an apartment downstairs, and that in the ten years of renting the space, she had never ever seen her. I thought that was kind of weird and really spooky.

"How does she get food?" I remember asking her.

"I honestly don't know," she answered. "My only contact with Miss Pierce is by email."

"By the way, she has a couple of rules, and she's very strict about them."

"What are the rules?" I asked the lady.

"No pets, and restrict your use of the house to the second floor."

I turned to Dad and said, "This sounds like a perfect setup for a murder mystery."

"Charlotte," he said, laughing. "I know this isn't the parent or author thing to say, but you need to stop reading so much. The poor woman is just a shy recluse … period."

"OK, Dad, but do you think she'll ever let us into the cool Tower on the top?"

"First, Charlotte, it's a cupola, not a Tower. Towers come on castles. This is just an architectural decoration on top of a Victorian house."

This is why my dad will always be a semi-famous travel writer and I will write great novels. No offense, Dad.

"Second, Charlotte," Dad interrupted my thoughts, his voice now serious. "We've been given two rules, and two rules only. If Miss Pierce wanted us on the third floor, she would have told the housing office. So, before we sign this lease, I need your assurance that you understand the rules — that means no exploring."

"I understand, Dad," I grumbled. What a waste of a tower, I thought.

Later, after I found out more about Miss Pierce, I got even more spooked. Yuri told me he'd been delivering to the back door since the eighties and he'd never seen her, either. She used to mail in all her checks, but now she does everything online. How interesting — a wired hermit.

My stomach growled, so I jumped off the swing and went back across the street. How bad could this sleepover be? I wondered. But that's what I'd thought about the first day of school.

I worried about what all the girls would think. Maeve lived above a movie theater and could watch free movies any time she wanted. Katani's house was full of people laughing and talking all the time. She might think our house was empty, boring, and creepy. Besides, when her grandmother asked where we lived and I told her 173 Summit Avenue, she gave me a really strange look. And Avery, who's always asking a million questions, would want to know what my mother died of and how old she was. This sleepover was already feeling like a big mistake.

Those are the two questions people always ask. The answers, "Pneumonia" and "32," have so little to do with my mother. I'd much rather tell them how she read to me all the time, how we rode the swan boats together, and how she smelled of lavender. She met my Dad in the Arboretum in spring when the lilacs were blooming. How romantic was that? But they never ask about those things.

Suddenly, out charged Dad with a big grin on his face, jolting me back to reality.

"Who's ready for pancakes?" he asked.

Then the day kind of kept moving after that, between the diner and the supermarket, and, can you believe it, even more cleaning.

CR

Dad had been monkeying about for ages, starting a fire and putting out more things for the s'mores. Don't ask me how it took so long, because there's only three things in s'mores. Katani was the first to show up, and I was actually glad, because it meant Dad had to stop making me nervous.

I could hear Kelley singing "This Old Man" as they pulled into the driveway.

"Shush!" said Katani.

But Kelley was un-shushable. "How's my new best friend?" she shouted, her head hanging out the window like a puppy dog.

"I'm great, Kelley. How are you?"

"I'm supercalifragilisticexpialidocious," she said.

"Shhh," said Katani, jumping out of the car. She wore black pants and a black and white striped top. Even for a sleepover, she looked perfect—trés chic.

Mrs. Fields leaned on the top of the car, looking at Katani and me and the house. She seemed quiet. "I've always loved this house," she said.

I thought she was just being nice, but her eyes actually

❀

❁

looked all misty.

"I mean it," she said, patting my hand. "This is a 'good times' house."

What did that mean? My dad came out and walked over to Mrs. Fields with big steps.

"Mrs. Fields," he said, "thank you so much for welcoming Charlotte to the Abigail Adams Junior High. It means so much to me that she's in such capable and understanding hands."

I went back around the car to Katani, to help her with her things. Wow. I didn't know girls my age carried suitcases to sleepovers. She wouldn't look me in the eye ... this was starting out well.

"Do you have many renters?" she asked, as we walked to the porch.

"No," I said.

"You mean, you have this whole house to yourself?" Her perfect eyebrows arched in surprise.

"Pretty much," I said. The words just popped out. I've never told even a semi-lie before. I couldn't believe this was me talking.

"We just don't use the rooms down here. It's nicer upstairs." We climbed the stairs and put her things in the living room. I knew I was giving the wrong impression, like we owned the house, but I couldn't help myself.

The bell rang, so I went back down. Dad came hustling down right after me. He opened the front door for Ms. Kaplan. Maeve's mom looked a little freaked because he was holding a barbecue fork.

"Don't worry! It's not a weapon!" he said, waving it around his head, laughing when he saw the look on her face. "It's for marshmallows! I'm Charlotte's dad, Richard Ramsey.

We take our s'mores very seriously around these parts."

"I'm Carol Kaplan," she said and cleared her throat.

They chatted for a minute as Maeve carried her duffel in. I could tell Ms. Kaplan was checking Dad out to make sure he wasn't crazy. She still didn't look convinced as she went down the porch steps.

"Maeve, is your cell phone charged?"

"Yes, Mom, don't worry," said Maeve, who was practicing sweeping gestures on the big inner staircase. Too many old movies.

"I want you to check in with me before you go to sleep."

"We're going to bed in about five minutes, Mom," groaned Maeve. "What could possibly happen to us between now and then?"

It looked like Ms. Kaplan was worried about exactly what *could* happen between now and then, but she settled on, "Call me. And no junk food after you brush your teeth."

As Dad was closing the door, Avery bounced through.

"Hi, Mr. Ramsey," she said. "I'm Avery."

"My pleasure, Avery. Won't you come in?"

"But I already am in," she said with a laugh and dashed up the stairs, sprinting around Maeve, who was practicing swooning over the banister.

Katani stood at the railing at the top of the stair, shaking her head as she watched Maeve.

A few moments later, Avery came rocketing down the banister at full speed.

The girls trooped into the living room. Dad had his African masks, an old map of Paris, and one ratty-looking butterfly net hanging on the wall. Dad and I had pulled the chairs and couch back from the fireplace and moved the coffee table off to one side. There was lots of space in the big room to sit on cushions around the fire and have all the snacks and drinks handy. It really helped that Dad had made a crackling fire in the huge, open fireplace. It gave us something to focus on as we sat awkwardly, not saying a word. Even he started to notice.

"Charlotte," Dad said, "let's get this party started."

"Sure thing, Dad," I said, as the girls rolled their eyes.

"How about some s'mores?" he said a bit too loudly.

He put a tray of Graham crackers, chocolate bars, and marshmallows on the coffee table.

I ran to the kitchen and brought back the fruit I had cut up for the girls, a bowl brimming with fresh strawberries, watermelon, and raspberries.

"My specialty," I said, trying to make a joke. "I call it 'Bowl of Red Fruit.'"

Nobody laughed except Dad. He was beginning to see what I was up against.

"Well, then," he said, clearing his throat. "I'll just leave you four alone to have fun."

He handed each of us a long, barbecue fork.

"Woo hoo!" said Avery, skewering five marshmallows at once. "Watch this!"

Within seconds, all five marshmallows were in flames and Avery was totally proud of herself.

"Honestly," sighed Katani. "Do you have a fire extinguisher handy somewhere?"

"What?" Avery said. "Are these bad?"

We all started to giggle.

Slowly, between the challenge of not frying our marshmallows and the pleasure of biting into gooey chocolate, I began to relax. Dad must have planned it this way, because while we were stuffing ourselves with s'mores, he had turned down the lights in the living room and snuck out.

As we huddled together around the fire, I imagined for a moment that we were friends. Then, Katani spoke.

"The sooner we go to bed, the sooner this will all be over."

Oh well, the friendship fantasy just went out the window.

CR

We each picked a spot around the living room to spread out our things. Katani opened her suitcase, which was tan with brown fabric around the edges. Everything in it was neat. She carefully took out a pair of blue satin pajamas. Suddenly, something flew past my eyes.

"Ow!" said Katani rubbing her neck and pulling a rubber band from Avery's braces out of her hair.

Avery burst out laughing.

"What are you doing?" asked Katani. "You're like an electric yo-yo."

"I didn't mean to get you, Katani, honest," said Avery. "I was aiming at Maeve."

"Glad you missed," Maeve said as she unpacked a few things. "Katani," she asked, "did you make those pajamas yourself?"

Katani stopped unrolling her sleeping bag long enough to lock Maeve in a cold stare.

"Why?"

"Oh, just wondering," said Maeve not looking up.

She put on headphones and started thumbing through a movie magazine. Katani walked slowly toward where Maeve lay on her sleeping bag. Uh-oh. Katani leaned over and flipped the power button off on Maeve's MP3 player. Maeve looked annoyed.

"Excuse me. Do you need something?"

"Yes, little princess," said Katani, her eyes blazing. "I'd like to see *your* pajamas."

Maeve looked from Katani to Avery and back to me, shrugging her shoulders.

"Sure. Whatever. What's the big deal?"

She pulled a light pink night shirt from her bag.

"Did you make those pajamas, Maeve?"

"Excuse me?"

"Or did you whine until Mommy and Daddy bought you that sixty dollar designer night shirt?"

"Katani ..." I thought I should say something to help Maeve. But Maeve was holding her own.

"Guess again," said Maeve. "For your information they were only nine dollars at Filene's Basement."

"I see," said Katani. "And the Louis Vuitton bag?"

"Louis, who?" piped up Avery. No one answered.

"You mean this old thing?" asked Maeve, posing like a model with her bag covered with little gold initials.

"Yeah," said Katani, getting heated up.

"It's a knockoff, Katani. A fake. I got it on Orchard Street in New York when we went to visit my grandparents."

"Whoa," said Avery, looking at me. "This is getting a little intense."

Katani kept going like she didn't even hear Avery.

"Well I'll bet you didn't find your laptop at Filene's Basement or on Orchard Street. How much did *that* cost?"

"You don't quit, do you?" asked Maeve, looking mad. "What's the big deal about the laptop? And by the way, what is with your attitude?"

"My attitude?" said Katani. "I guess it's not a big deal for a spoiled, rich kid to carry a fifteen-hundred-dollar laptop, when the school supplies pens and paper."

Maeve was furious.

"If you knew the real reason," she screamed, "maybe you wouldn't be so mean, you witch."

Suddenly Maeve burst into tears.

"You wouldn't know what it's like to have a learning disability, would you?" Maeve cried. "If you must know, I'm dyslexic. It's hard to read and even harder to write. The laptop makes writing easier. And, yes, Miss Perfect, my *Mommy* got *special* permission for her *special* daughter to use the laptop in class. And I get extra time for tests too. My mother drives me to lessons, calls me every ten minutes, and wants me to floss. So you can tease me about my laptop all you want, but the last thing I am is spoiled. I've never bought anything full price in my life. I have over-protective parents, an obnoxious brother, and no space of my own. You're so perfect you probably never had a problem in your life."

"Why does everyone think my life is so perfect?" demanded Katani, her hands on her hips.

"Because you look like a supermodel?" suggested Avery.

"Let me tell you all something. The only thing perfect in my house is my two older sisters. You try living with two brilliant, superstar athletes! And don't even try to talk to me about disabilities. I have an autistic sister I have to share a room with and protect every day of the week."

Maeve looked shocked. "You do?"

"That's right!" she answered fiercely.

"What's wrong with being artistic?" Avery asked.

"Oh, for Pete's sake, Avery," groaned Katani. "She's *autistic*, not *artistic*. Never mind. It's too hard to explain."

"She's really sweet and cute," I added to be helpful.

Katani turned on me.

"Like you care, Charlotte! People like you make me so

mad. You come to my house, act sweet and innocent, get in good with my grandmother, and then you go back to school and make jokes about Kelley!"

"What?" I gasped. "How can you say that? I've never made a joke about her. I loved being with Kelley and Patrice and your grandmother. I loved being with everyone in your family except YOU! You were a real ..." I stopped in time before saying something I would regret.

"Katani, you were totally mean to me too," added Avery. "You acted like being adopted is bad, or something. News Flash: I'm adopted."

"You are?" Maeve asked.

"Sure," she said proudly. "Avery Madden here. Born in Seoul, South Korea, October 30, 1991. Arrived home four months later on Valentine's Day."

Avery's newsflash was like a mini cease-fire. For a second, everyone stopped fighting.

"You completely misunderstood me, Avery," said Katani. "I'm not against adoption. I was just mad at you for being so rude about me not having the sports talent of my sisters. Anyway, this is off the point. We were talking about Charlotte."

"I totally agree with you, Katani," said Maeve, blowing her nose loudly. "Charlotte does have that sweet and innocent act down perfectly."

"What are you talking about?" I said. "Are you people all crazy?"

Instead of answering, Maeve snatched my glasses off the end table and put them on.

"Here's another impersonation. Who am I? 'Yoo-hoo, Nick, darling. Let me tell you about my fabulous travels around the world while I steal you from Maeve.'"

Steal Nick from Maeve? What was this girl talking about?

"Don't give me that wide-eyed look like you don't know what I mean!"

"Tell her, girl," chimed in Katani.

"But, Maeve," I stammered, "I *don't* know what you mean."

Avery imitated phone static and said, "We are presently experiencing technical difficulties."

"Avery, shush," said Maeve.

"You saw I liked Nick on the first day of school!"

"I did not!"

"Must need new glasses," said Katani under her breath.

"Maeve," I said "you flirt with all the boys."

"But in Montoya's," said Maeve, "you kept trying to get all his attention."

"I didn't want his attention." Tears welled up in my eyes. "Believe me. I don't need anyone's attention."

"Wow!" said Avery. "I'd love to see what would happen if you did. As long as I wasn't too close."

"Avery ..." said Katani.

"Avery ..." said Maeve.

"Avery ..." I said.

"... SHUT UP!" we all screamed at once.

"Is everything always a joke to you?" asked Maeve, turning on Avery.

"Do you always have to laugh at other people's problems?" I added.

Avery looked crushed.

"Don't you know how to act around people?" said Katani, towering over her.

Avery crumpled to the floor and put her arms around her knees. "I know how to act around some people," she said, wiping a tear with the back of her hand. "Just not you people." Suddenly, rough-and-rugged Avery looked small and helpless. I knew how she felt.

"I don't know what they're talking about half the time either, Avery. Every time I move I have to try and figure out what everybody is talking about ... it's really hard," I said.

Avery sighed and stretched out on the floor. Katani sat down beside her. It was like the quiet after a hurricane.

Maeve cleared her throat. "Did you really make your pajamas, Katani?"

"Uh-oh," said Avery crawling for a corner. "Oh no! Here we go again."

"I like them," blurted Maeve. "I, the Queen of Designer Discount Shopping, have never seen anything like them."

"I sew a lot of my own clothes," said Katani quietly.

"Seriously?" Maeve gasped. "The striped top?"

Katani nodded.

"That black skirt?"

"Uh-huh."

"That would be the 'first day' striped top?" I asked.

"Yup. Two weeks babysitting, four fabric stores, special silk foot for the sewing machine, and three days to sew. And you took it out in under thirty seconds."

"Oh, Katani," I said, feeling terrible all over again, "I'm so sorry. Really, I am."

"Girl, you should be," she snorted. "By the way, have you considered klutz insurance?" She was laughing when she said it.

Maeve came over to sit next to her.

"Maeve," said Katani, "I'm sorry I called you a princess."

"And I'm sorry I said you were Miss Perfect," said Maeve.

"Hey, you guys," said Avery, "Now you're acting like a

bunch of girls."

"Avery," I said. "News Flash: We ARE Girls."

"No matter how short one of us may be," added Katani.

That was all it took. Avery jumped up, grabbed a cushion from the couch, and threw it at Katani's head. Katani ducked and it hit Maeve. The next thing I knew, couch cushions were flying and we were bashing each other with pillows and choking with laughter.

"Everything all right in there?" yelled my dad from down the hall.

"Perfect!" I called as a pillow knocked my legs completely out from under me.

This might work out, after all.

❧

PART TWO

BEST FRIENDS

CHAPTER 15

Charlotte

NIGHT SAFARI

I WOKE WHEN THE SHIP'S CLOCK on the mantle struck two. Our roaring fire was glowing embers now. The moon, nearly full, shone through the window. While the others slept, I lay on my back staring at shadows dancing on the wall. Out the window, above the trees, I could see the stars. And inside, in sleeping bags scattered around the room, were Katani, Avery, and Maeve ... just maybe ... my new friends.

A faint scritch scratch noise had been going on for awhile without my really noticing. Maybe because Avery was snoring like a three-hundred-pound gorilla. Then I realized that the scritching wasn't stopping. I tried as best I could to aim my flashlight before I turned it on. When I did, the light shone on a bag of candy next to sleeping Maeve. Nothing odd about that. Then the bag wiggled. Two beady eyes peered out of the bag, red in the flashlight beam. I couldn't believe it—a mouse!

I flipped off the light. A moment of terror. Would the girls think the house was infested with rodents? Maeve moved in her sleep. She rolled onto her back. I prayed she wouldn't wake up.

The mouse left the bag, crept across the floor, and onto Maeve's hair. I knew I had to wake her.

"Maeve," I called in the calmest whisper I could manage.

"Hmm," she answered groggily.

Then I uttered the two most useless words in the English language: "Don't panic."

"Why? What's wrong?" She sat bolt upright. The mouse fell in her lap. "Aaaaaaaah!" Maeve let out a blood-curdling shriek. "A mouse! Help!" Terrified, the mouse was already scampering to the next sleeping bag.

"What is wrong with you?" groused Katani, waking from a deep sleep as the mouse scampered onto her bare arm.

"Eeew!!" she shrieked, flinging it in the hallway.

Avery was wide awake and ready for adventure.

"Yo!" she yelled, grabbing Dad's butterfly net and chasing the mouse across the floor and into the hall. "Come on, girls! It's time for a big game hunt!"

Maeve and I were up and ready for the chase. Maeve reached for one of Dad's safari hats.

"I feel like Katharine Hepburn in *The African Queen*," Maeve gestured dramatically. What was that girl talking about now?

"Whatever," said Katani, rolling over and covering her ears with her hands.

I picked up my digital camera from the coffee table. Maeve grabbed it and took a picture of herself. "I really hate mice but this could make a thrilling adventure story."

"Come on!" called Avery from the hall, but Katani wouldn't budge.

"No way am I running after some filthy rodent in the middle of the night! What's the matter with you people?"

She laughed at us hovering over her in our ridiculous gear.

"I know how to get her up," said Maeve. She turned a light on and pointed the camera at Katani. "Meet the star of our adventure, 12-year-old Katani Summers—student by day and world-famous rodent hunter by night."

Katani covered her face and her hair. "Don't you dare take my picture, Maeve," she said, trying to grab the camera. "If anyone saw me like this I'd have to move. I'm up. I'm up already. See me get up."

"Vanity. The world's most powerful weapon," Maeve said, whispering in my ear.

We crept down the dark-paneled hall as Maeve imitated a laugh from a horror movie and said, "For four unsuspecting girls, a night that began as a simple sleepover was about to turn ugly."

"Shhh!" said Katani. "You'll wake up Charlotte's father."

"Don't worry about him," I said. "I've seen him sleep through an elephant stampede."

"Shhhhh!" whispered Avery. "How can we track big game with you people talking?" She led the way with a flashlight and net.

"Avery, you're insane," said Katani from the rear. "Who wants a mouse, anyway?"

"I collect small animals," she whispered. "I have a frog, three toads, and some other stuff."

"Glad we didn't sleep over at your house," said Katani.

"I'd rather have a dog, or anything with fur, but Mom's allergic," explained Avery. "Adding a mouse to my collection would be great. I'll just have to keep him away from Walter. He loves to strangle mice and then swallow them head first."

"Who's Walter?" I asked, horrified.

"My snake," said Avery.

"Eeeew!" squawked Maeve and Katani. "Snakes are really disgusting!"

"Shhh!" said Avery again. We tiptoed across the Oriental carpet and down the hall.

"Hold this," whispered Avery, handing me the net. "The mouse is heading for the vent!"

She dashed ahead with the flashlight; we caught her kneeling and pointing her light into the brass heating vent.

"Whither the dragon?" asked Maeve.

"Huh?" Avery asked. "Maeve, are you OK?"

"Where's your creativity," asked Maeve, "Would you rather be chasing a dragon, or a mouse?"

"Rats!" said Avery.

"Where?!" I said, jumping back. "Yikes!"

Avery burst out laughing.

"Charlotte, it's just an expression."

"I knew that."

"It's gone," said Avery. "Down the heating duct to the basement, and maybe outside."

She sounded really disappointed.

"There were always huge rats on the docks in Paris," I muttered, shuddering.

"Can we please go back to bed?" said Katani. "Now that the dragon has fled."

She managed to smirk at all three of us while she said it.

"What's that?" asked Avery as she moved the flashlight beam across the vent.

"It looks like a doorbell, Avery," I said quickly. "Just leave it alone."

"But Charlotte," said Avery, "since when do people put doorbells in heating vents?"

"Go ahead! Push it!" said Maeve excitedly.

"No, wait!" I begged. What if that doorbell rang downstairs and woke up the spooky landlady? What if it was some kind of alarm? I was getting in deep here—and the girls were really getting into the house. What are they going to do when they find out it's not mine? I better slow this train down.

Too late. Avery was already pushing the button. I felt sick. I strained my ears and thought I heard the faint sound of a bell echoing through the vent. But I couldn't be sure. I leaned my head closer. Suddenly, the sound of gears grinding overhead blocked out the sound of anything below.

"What's that?" asked Katani, flattening herself against the wall and throwing her hands over her head.

"Cool!" said Avery. "Wouldya look at that?"

"Yikes!" said Maeve, holding the brim of her safari hat.

The painted ceiling slid sideways, leaving the cherubs without their fluffy clouds. A black velvet cord dropped down from the ceiling.

"Whoa!" said Avery.

"This is like a movie I saw once!" cried Maeve, grabbing the velvet rope.

"Hold on!" I finally managed to say. "We've GOT to be really careful. My Dad didn't say I could go in this part of the house."

"Why not, Charlotte?" asked Katani.

"It's your house, too, isn't it?" asked Maeve.

"Well, yes," I gulped, "sort of, but ..."

Now I was completely trapped. I'd have to tell them everything. Either that or totally go against Dad. Tonight had been great. Finally, we were becoming friends. I could feel it. "I ..."

"Charlotte?"

"What? No, Avery, please, don't!" Too late. She was

already pulling the cord.

"Maybe you shouldn't," said Katani in a worried voice.

"How can we not?" said Maeve, rushing to help Avery. "Think *Indiana Jones!* Think *Raiders of the Lost Ark!*"

As the girls pulled, a shaft of moonlight shone on steep wooden stairs. It was practically a ladder and it was sliding down from the ceiling.

"Come on!" said Avery, scampering up the stairs. Maeve was right behind her.

"You just let me know what you find," said Katani. "I'll guard the ladder."

"Oh no you don't," said Maeve. "We're all in this together." She came back down the ladder and tied the sash of Katani's bathrobe around her waist like a rock climber. "Now move it!" she said pulling a nervous Katani behind her. I knew I would be in a ton of trouble if Dad or Miss Pierce ever found out about this, but for now, there was nothing to do but follow. The truth is, I was excited too. I'd wanted to get into the Tower since the first day I'd seen it.

With each step, I rose through the opening in the floor. It seemed as if I was stepping into the sky. The windows were full of moon and stars. After all the wishing and waiting, it was hard to believe that the Tower was even better than I'd ever imagined. There was no way I could tell them this wasn't all ours ... not yet.

The four of us tiptoed around in the moonlight, speaking in hushed voices like we had entered some sacred cathedral. The view of the city lights took my breath away.

"It's so incredibly beautiful," Maeve gasped. "I'm at a total loss for words."

"That's something she doesn't say every day," said Avery, laughing.

Through the window straight ahead, the lights of Brookline melted into the lights of Boston, where skyscrapers sparkled and a giant red triangle flashed the word "CITGO."

"There's Fenway Park," said Avery, "That's where the Red Sox play, Charlotte," she explained.

Out the left window, the Charles River separated Boston and Cambridge. Katani pointed out Harvard University, and, farther along, MIT.

"That's Harvard Business School," she said, pointing to a dome in the distance. "See it just to the right of Memorial Stadium? That's where I'm going to get my business degree. I'm going to have my very own chain of fashion and advice centers someday."

Avery pointed out two soccer fields to the South. To the west, the Massachusetts Turnpike wound off in the distance.

"Red taillights head westward into the night," said Maeve, arms stretched toward the highway. "Next stop: Hollywood, California, where all my dreams will come true."

Katani spun around in a high, lime green swivel chair that looked like it came from the fifties or sixties.

"Why's this here, do you suppose?" she asked. "Hmm ... I could do some serious makeovers in this chair."

Maeve dusted off an oval mirror on a gold stand with her sleeve, and then stood speechless, twisting and turning, admiring herself.

"Oh," she sighed. "Oh, this is beautiful."

"Someone tell Nick not to bother," said Katani, while Avery and I pretended to gag. "Maeve has found her true love: Herself."

Even Maeve laughed. "It's the most fabulous mirror in the universe," she sighed again. "Look. The flecks in it make you shimmer."

"And she has the nerve to call *me* vain," said Katani.

"Ouch," I cried out, stubbing my toe on something. "Flash the light over here."

"Hey!" said Avery. "It's a big old desk."

Suddenly, Avery disappeared into the shadows. She had scrambled up an almost invisible ladder attached to the wall.

"Look at me," she shouted.

That was impossible, since she had managed to disappear through a small hole in the Tower roof.

"You guys!" came Avery's slightly muffled voice. "You have to come up here! It's a telescope, I think!"

That's all I needed to hear. I ran to the ladder to follow Avery. I stuck my head through the hole at the top. There was barely room for two of us on the platform that lay just below a domed metal roof. Avery knelt beside the most beautiful brass and gold telescope I'd ever seen. It had gizmos, gears, and all kinds of gadgets attached to it. I crawled over to check out the eyepiece.

"There's nothing to look at!" griped Avery.

We shone our lights around the room. It wasn't that hard to find the hand crank. Everything else in the room was attached to the telescope.

"Cool!" said Avery. "Let's try it!"

I'd worried about pushing the button in the vent, and climbing the ladder, and going into the Tower, but I HAD to find out how to use this telescope. I took a deep breath and turned the crank. Nothing. It didn't budge.

"C'mon," said Avery. "You can do it."

I tried again. The wheel squeaked and slowly began to turn. Avery and I stood in awe as the ceiling above us opened slowly. Above us, with no windows in between, was a ceiling of stars and the night. The metal room glowed in moonlight.

I was home.

"Yeah!!!!" Avery hollered at the top of her lungs.

"Hey!" called Katani. "It's getting cold in here! Did you open a window?"

"More like a door to the stars," I answered. "You have to come and see this!"

"If you think I'm climbing into some bird's nest in the dark, you're crazy!"

I started laughing. I, Charlotte Ramsey, had friends to share the stars with. I couldn't wait to teach them the constellations like my Dad had taught me.

Avery closed the roof and we climbed back into the Tower. Maeve had torn herself away from the mirror and found a light switch. With a "one, two, three" she turned it on.

"Maybe it just needs new bulbs," I hoped aloud.

"We can change them in the morning," said Avery.

The morning, I thought. What would I do about Dad and Miss Pierce? How could I manage to be here with my friends, and not let Dad or Miss Pierce know until I'd had a chance to straighten it out?

A PLACE OF OUR OWN

"Let's make the Tower our own secret ... best friends' apartment," said Avery.

"That would be sooo cool. Let's do it!" shouted Katani.

"Works for me," Maeve said.

"Think of it ... a space of our own. No older brothers allowed!" exclaimed Avery.

"No too-perfect-for-words older sisters," said Katani with a big smile.

"No violin teachers or little brothers!" shrieked Maeve.

I chimed in with "No Dad!" I felt guilty saying that, but

there was no way I could say what I was really thinking, which was "No more being lonely!" And seeing my new friends so excited made it really easy to forget the Tower wasn't mine.

"Can we decorate it?" asked Katani with a glint in her eye. I could tell she was already mentally measuring, placing furniture, and accessorizing.

"Sure," I said. "Why not? It's our apartment, isn't it?

"As long as we all swear nobody will ever know about it but us. Not even my Dad. We'll have to sneak in and out."

Okay, I thought. This might just work out until I sort everything out.

CHAPTER 16

Katani

LET'S DO LUNCH

BEFORE HOMEROOM, MAEVE, CHARLOTTE, AVERY, AND I met in the hall and made plans to go to the Tower that afternoon before Charlotte's dad got home at five. I already had a whole notebook of decorating ideas to share. I had spent all Sunday afternoon cutting out magazine pictures and making lists of how to divide and decorate our secret space.

"Hello, girls," said Ms. Rodriguez, sneaking up behind us. "How was your weekend?"

"Awesome!" said Avery.

"Great!" said Charlotte.

"Incredible!" said Maeve.

Ms. Rodriguez looked right at me.

"It was fine," I mumbled, out of earshot of the others. I had had the best time at the sleepover, but I didn't want to give her the satisfaction of saying, "I told you so."

"I'm so glad," she said.

In homeroom, Ms. Rodriguez handed back everyone's letter assignments except mine. She came over to my desk. "Do you think you and the girls will be wanting to change your lunch table assignment today?"

Before the weekend, I would have given my sewing machine to get away from those three. But the sleepover had changed all that. I had plans for my girls and I had plans for our new apartment. I cleared my throat. "Not just yet, Ms. Rodriguez. We were thinking it might not be fair to the other kids. We'll let you know when it feels like the right time."

"Thank you Katani. I think that's a good idea," said Ms. Rodriguez, with a pleased expression on her face. She gave us a few minutes to read her responses to our "If I could change a school rule ..." letters. Since she'd already talked about my letter at lunch on Friday, I worked on decorating ideas for the Tower. Avery seemed really happy with what Ms. R said about her changing-the-rules letter.

Avery Madden
School Rule Assignment:

Dear Ms. Rodriguez:
There are three things I would like to change about Junior High. If I'm elected Class President, I'll work on the first two. The last one seems like a lot of work, so maybe we could discuss it in Social Studies some time.

1. *We need snack time. (Just because you're in Junior High, doesn't mean your blood sugar doesn't drop.)*
2. *We need recess after lunch. (People need a break after 5 hours of sitting and listening!)*
3. *Every time we take one of those standardized tests (like the Reading Placement Test yesterday), we have to check a box for what we are:*

Asian ___	African American ___
Caucasian ___	Hispanic ___
Pacific Islander ___	Other ___

I was born in Korea, so I always check Asian, but my parents and brothers are Caucasian, so sometimes I feel like an Other. It's so confusing. It makes me mad that I have to decide. Everyone is an individual. What about the kids who are a mix of two boxes? Do they check both boxes or Other? Who wants to be an Other anyway? My solution is to get rid of all those boxes. Also, even though it says "optional," you feel like you should check a box, and then you start wondering about the boxes. And then you get distracted from the test. And, what if you make a mistake and check the wrong box? Do they come and arrest you, or what?

Sincerely,

Avery Madden

☙

Dear Avery,

Thank you for your suggestions. You have taken this assignment to the next level by suggesting change that affects more lives than your own. I hope you won't mind if I use your letter as an example for the class on how letter writing can make a difference. I think the topic of "Other" would be a great discussion item for Social Studies, and I'll suggest it to Mr. Danson.

Great work!

Sincerely,

Ms. Rodriguez

Charlotte Ramsey
School Rule Assignment:

Dear Ms. Rodriguez,
I am very disappointed that only 8th and 9th graders
are allowed to be on the school paper. You know, a great
many 7th graders have important things to say. And some
7th graders may be really good writers, as well. I would like
to propose that we have a special section in the school
newspaper devoted entirely to the 7th grade—created,
written and produced by our class. By having our own page,
we would feel more a part of the school, and less like "the
new kids on the block."
Sincerely,
Charlotte Ramsey

❧

Dear Charlotte,
Charlotte, you raise a very valid point. I don't know
when and how that rule started, but I promise to look into
it with Ms. Knowland and get back to you.
Thank you for your creative suggestions. Perhaps,
you can begin to think about how you might get other
students involved, and what that page might look like.
Sincerely,
Ms. Rodriguez

Maeve Kaplan-Taylor
School Rule Assignment:

Dear Ms. Rodriguez,
I think junior high would be way better
if dance music was piped in first thing
during homeroom. My two reasons are:

1. *60 Minutes* did a story that showed
   that teenagers have a hard time
   functioning before 10 a.m. And, they
   didn't even bother to test kids like
   me who have a hard time functioning
   before noon. But I can tell you one
   thing for sure. 7:50 a.m. is absolutely
   impossible for everybody at this
   school. I have personally seen people
   asleep, with disgusting drool coming
   out of their mouths many times during
   morning announcements (Henry, Dirk,
   Amber, FYI ...)

2. Great music could put us in a better
   mood for first period, so we're ready
   to learn. In fact, I have never seen a
   person in a good mood during first
   period—except for Betsy Fitzgerald,
   who acts like she's perfect. (And, I
   don't think the rest of us should have
   to live up to that.)

Sincerely,
Maeve Kaplan-Taylor
P.S. I would be more than happy to
volunteer as DJ.

Dear Maeve,

I see your point about music as a way to pep up students first thing in the morning. I can assure you, there's nothing more depressing than facing a room full of blank stares during first period. I would like to have you "DJ" the morning announcements on a trial basis. Let's plan your debut for a special occasion when your music and what you have to say will be a celebration of something important. I'll let you know when.

Sincerely,

Ms. Rodriguez

ख

After Ms. Rodriguez handed back all of our suggestions for changing a school rule, she said it was important that we spend some time talking about them as a class. "Does anyone want to comment about what it felt like to imagine changing a school rule?" she asked, standing in front of the class, half-sitting on her desk.

Betsy Fitzgerald's hand shot up. "I really enjoyed this assignment," she said.

Dillon Johnson groaned. "It figures," he hissed to Pete.

Ms. Rodriguez gave Dillon a warning look. "I want everyone to feel free to speak what's on his or her mind. Please, no put-downs," she said firmly.

"Rules are important, though," Betsy continued. "I bet the school has to think long and hard about all sorts of things." She smiled a little primly. "It's like my dad always says—if we didn't have red lights, people could just drive through intersections and kill each other. And then where would we be?"

Pete snorted, and Ms. Rodriguez put her hand up. "Betsy

has a point. A society needs rules. Rules are one way that we agree about how we're going to live together. But on the other hand, sometimes rules get outgrown ... or dated ... and it's up to us to think about whether or not they need changing."

Joline's hand shot up. "I think we need more privileges. Lots of middle schools start in sixth grade. Just because we're the youngest class here doesn't mean we're babies. Some of us are thirteen!"

"I hear your concern, Joline," Ms. Rodriguez said mildly. "Any other thoughts?"

"Some rules make sense," Nick Montoya remarked. "Others seem ... I don't know, like they're just there for the sake of being, you know, rules. Like we should just have rules."

"I like that comment," Ms. Rodriguez smiled. "I noticed, when I was reading through your suggestions, that some of you suggested changes that would affect you personally." A few people looked a little sheepish. "Some of you tried to think about the bigger community, too. Both are OK," she added. "And part of the point of this exercise was to get all of you to start thinking together as a community. What rules do you value? Which ones do you want to work together to change? Remember, it's a lot harder to change a rule than to put one in place. If you care about making a difference, you're going to have to figure out a way to work as a team."

Anna shot Joline a look which clearly said "yuck." I liked what Ms. Rodriguez was saying, though. Better yet, I liked the fact that she was clearly listening to us when we talked. And she didn't seem to have made her mind up yet about what she thought. I liked that too.

CHAPTER 17

Katani

THE FOUR CORNERS

MY PARENTS SAY I SHOULD HOST one of those TV shows where you make over someone's house while they're out getting coffee. I redecorate Kelley's and my room all the time.

As soon as school was over, we all rushed to Charlotte's. Pulling my wheelie-bag full of supplies up the hill was a killer, especially in high boots. By the time we got there, I was a mess.

The front hall was quiet and empty, just like Saturday night. I didn't get it. Why would anyone have such a beautiful downstairs dining room and living room and not use them? If that were my mahogany table and crystal chandelier, we'd be eating there every night.

Once in the Tower, the girls didn't exactly follow my directions. When I told them we had to clean, Maeve cranked up the music and kept lip-syncing, using the broom as a pretend microphone. Avery tied dust rags on her sneakers and skated in circles. Charlotte couldn't bring herself to leave the telescope platform.

I was getting frustrated. I put my hands on my hips,

snatched the broom from Maeve, and blurted out, "Unless we get rid of these cobwebs, we'll have spiders in our hair!" That did the trick. Team Clean got to work.

After a while, the place smelled great and in spite of the fooling around, the Tower was really coming together. Charlotte had polished the telescope until it was so shiny I could have used it for a makeup mirror. I had to give that girl credit; she had even put sachets she made out of French lavender in every corner.

"Now for the real fun," I said, opening up my bag.

Avery ran over. "Got any food in there?"

She wrinkled her nose when I pulled out some fabric for my window. "What's that frilly stuff?"

"Window treatment," I said.

"No treats?" she asked, disappointed.

I stood in the center of the room and announced, "There are four windows, four window seats, and four of us."

"Destiny!" said Maeve, putting her hand on her forehead and striking a dramatic pose. "West!" she said. "I want a view towards sunsets, and Hollywood."

"I don't get it, Maeve. Why do you want to go to Hollywood anyway? And why be a movie star? It's so ... shallow," Avery shrugged. "I don't know. All they think about is what they look like and how much money they get paid. It's kinda sick."

Maeve was opening and closing her cell phone, as if she had an imaginary agent on the line. "That's not how it's going to be for me. I'm not in it for the money. I just love to perform! And, it's not so easy. Have you ever tried to totally act like someone else? Plus, I'm going to be one of those super compassionate movie stars, like Audrey Hepburn. You know, when she got famous, she traveled all over the world helping poor, starving kids?" Her eyes were shining. "Audrey Hepburn is the best. I loved her in *Sabrina*. That's my favorite story on earth. When she came back from Paris all sophisticated and beautiful ..."

Avery rolled her eyes. "So what does sophisticated have to do with helping kids?"

Maeve looked indignant. "Not Sabrina, silly. She's just a character. But the real Audrey Hepburn was amazing. She was a famous actress and she helped poor kids all over the world ... for the United Nations. Like Angelina Jolie. She does that too."

"Yeah?" Avery didn't look completely convinced.

"I'm going to do that too. In fact I'm going to get started on the helping-people-out part first," Maeve said suddenly. "It's never too early. Then when I'm famous I can just keep it going. And people will know it's the real deal because I will have been doing it for so long."

Maeve was really getting excited. She twirled around. "I know I can't really travel around the world yet. But there's still a lot I could do around here."

"There is?" Avery looked skeptical.

"Definitely! I could ... I could ... I'll think of something," Maeve stopped still, deep in thought. "I will, you'll see."

Avery snorted. "Maeve saves the world while she becomes the star of stage and screen."

"Don't be so negative, Avery! I'm serious! There are homeless people, sick kids ... old people. They need our help. They really do. It could be so great! You know, kids our age working together to help people in need." Her eyes shone.

I laughed. "Girl, I can hear you now. Oprah's going to love this."

Maeve looked defensive. "OK, ok. Go ahead and make

fun of me. But, you just wait. You guys are going to be all over this once I get this going."

I pointed her toward the window to the left at the top of the stairs. I'd already chosen the one I wanted: The view of the Charles River behind the dome of "The Business School." Some day I'm going to go there. Only my Grandma knows that I've already planned out my business. I'm going to start a chain of personal advice and fashion makeover centers for busy women. I've even started to build a website with tips for bringing out everyone's inner beauty. As I always say, it's all about attitude.

Avery parked herself on the window seat overlooking Corey Hill Park.

"Hey you guys!" she yelled. "Look at this! I can see the soccer fields! Cool! You're not covering this up with those window treats. Stay away, Katani."

Charlotte let the rest of us go first. But she seemed happy with the window that was left: a view to the skyscrapers of downtown Boston. The sun glinted off the glass of the Hancock Tower. Beyond that sparkled the Atlantic Ocean. You could even see the runways of Logan Airport and a plane taking off.

"Perfect for you, Global Girl," I said.

"It *is* totally perfect," she whispered. "Over near that gold dome of the State House are the swan boats my mother used to take me to in the Boston Public Gardens when I was little. I still have the picture from her."

I couldn't imagine not having a mother. Even though my mom's a lawyer and works all the time, she's never missed tucking me in, no matter how late she gets home.

"Let's decorate Charlotte's area first," I said. "What do you want up here?"

Charlotte's green eyes lit up.

"My writing supplies!" she said. "I love writing with a beautiful view in front of me."

"You got it," I said. "Come on girls."

How hard could it be to get writing supplies up here? Famous last words. The drawers in her desk were labeled: Writing Materials, Chocolate Stash, Journals, and Jewelry Making Stuff. Each one overflowed with Charlotte's treasures. I'd never seen so many different kinds of chocolate from bits to bars to kisses.

"What are you planning to do," I asked, "open up Charlotte's candy store?"

"Yum!" said Avery.

"Pour moi?" asked Maeve biting into a Godiva chocolate.

The jewelry drawer was loaded with sea glass from Australia, beads from Africa, and ribbons and buttons from France. What a pack rat. She must have had ten journals, every color fountain pen, as many ink bottles as I have nail polishes, and also sealing wax, stamp pads, markers, airplane barf bags, and bulging scrapbooks.

When we had filled bags with everything from the drawers and carried them to the Tower, Charlotte said, "I can't wait to start writing."

"Honey," I said, "You better write the next *Harry Potter* after what it took to get all that stuff up here."

"Whoops," she said. "Forgot one thing."

"Nooooooooo!" said Maeve. "No more!"

"Don't worry. I'll get it myself."

She ran downstairs and came back wearing a stylin' vintage denim jacket.

"My lucky writing jacket," she said.

I tacked up silk fabric above my window, and then I lined

up my nail polishes, from clear to midnight blue, on my window seat. That swivel chair would make a great makeover center, a great place to launch the business I'd always dreamed of. Maybe I could even make up some business cards someday.

Avery lay on her stomach on her window seat, twiddling her thumbs, and looking out the window. "Next time, I'm bringing my Nerf basketball hoop so I can practice."

"Well, I'm going to make this whole area in front of my window a stage," said Maeve.

"There's a surprise," I said.

Maeve ignored me. She was busy lip-syncing.

Charlotte was trying to attach something to the wall beside her window but was struggling with the tape.

"No wonder," I said, ripping her a piece. "You don't have any fingernails."

"I got the idea of hanging quotes the day I was in your grandmother's office," Charlotte said.

I was quiet. Now that we were friends, I was feeling a little guilty about how I had treated her that day. "Here, let me hang it up for you," I said.

"Thanks, Katani."

"No problem. What's it mean anyway?" I asked. It was written in French and English:

Les yeux sont aveugles; il faut chercher avec le coeur.
The eyes are blind; one must search with the heart.

—Saint-Exupéry

"It's from a book called *The Little Prince*," Charlotte said. "I read it in France, but they also have it here, at the Book Nook in English."

I didn't know exactly what it meant but it reminded me of Charlotte. You had to look past her glasses and her disasters to appreciate her. She was like her house. They both had great bones. They just needed me to redecorate.

"Hey, Maeve!" called Avery from the telescope platform. "I can see your mom. She's running out of the movie theater. That's so cool ..."

Maeve stopped dancing on top of the window seat.

"Now she's getting into the car."

"Oh my gosh," said Maeve, looking at her watch. "I'm late for Hebrew School."

Just then her phone started playing "Tomorrow" from the musical *Annie*.

"Yes, Mom. Sorry. I know. I'll meet you at the bottom of Corey Hill in about two minutes."

Maeve air-kissed Charlotte on both cheeks.

"Au revoir, ma cherie."

"Au revoir, Maeve. How did you learn to speak French?" asked Charlotte.

"From the movies ... I learn everything from the movies!" said Maeve.

"And don't forget her role model, Miss Piggy, speaks French," joked Avery.

"I'll squash you later," laughed Maeve. "Ciao!"

"Bye, Maeve," we all shouted as our dramatic friend clattered down the stairs.

"I gotta go too," said Avery. "Soccer practice."

"Can you stay, Katani?" asked Charlotte.

"Just to write up my decorating To Do list. Then I want to catch the 'T' before people start coming home from work. I hate being packed in a crowded subway car like a sardine."

Decorating To Do List:

1. Bring Windex and paper towels to polish mirror
2. Bring neck cushion for makeover chair
3. Bring extra pair of heels for teaching the girls how to walk with attitude
4. Bring makeover emergency kit ... just in case.

𝒦

CHAPTER 18

Avery

COUNTDOWN TO THE WEEKEND

2:09. 2:10. 2:11. WOULD THE BELL EVER RING? Would the weekend ever get here? I couldn't wait to sleep over at Charlotte's again. For a week we'd been going to the Tower whenever we were free. My practices and Maeve's lessons were major road blocks. That kid takes more lessons than anyone I ever met in my life.

Mr. Moore was droning on and on and on. "The color of leaves is determined by the process of photosynthesis ..."

Why couldn't we roll around in the leaves instead of talking about them? He sounded like he was holding his nose when he talked.

"What is the function of chlorophyll?"

Maeve was clicking away on her laptop, taking notes. If it were me, I'd probably be playing solitaire. I can't believe how hard she works.

"I'm going to be passing back the quizzes on scientific methods and theories now," he said. "A few of you did exceptionally well." As he shuffled along the rows, handing out papers, I leaned forward in my seat to check out people's

✿

grades. Henry Yurt had failed again but he at least he was improving. Last quiz he got a zero. This time he got a 2. Must have remembered to sign his name.

"Sit down, please, Avery. Other people's test scores are their own business."

Who was he kidding? Didn't he know the first thing everyone did was compare grades? I looked at Maeve's. Ouch! "75," when she'd spent a whole afternoon in the Tower getting ready for it with Charlotte. All I'd done was shoot baskets and I got an "89."

"Avery," said Mr. Moore. "Please stop clicking your pen in and out or I'll have to take it away."

But as Mr. Moore turned to the board, my pen came apart and the spring and ink cartridge shot across the room. Then the bell rang.

Finally! I scrambled to get my pen guts back and get out of school.

CHAPTER 19

Avery

DISCOVERY

I SAW IT FIRST. I was juggling a Hackeysack around the Tower when Katani barked at me to quit or I'd ruin Maeve's freshly painted green toenails. Big green deal!

"Do you ever sit still?" griped Katani.

"Not if I can help it," I answered.

But I figured I'd give her a break, so I climbed up to the telescope where Charlotte was stargazing. It was fun annoying Katani, but I didn't want to push it. Well, not too much. I lay down near the opening at the top of the ladder and fired a few rubber bands off my braces at Katani. She'd tuned me out like my brothers do.

"Whatcha' lookin' at, Charlotte?" I asked.

"I was trying to find Ursa Major, the big bear, but it's kind of cloudy tonight, so I'm not having much luck."

"Let's look at Fenway Park!" I suggested and swung the telescope in the direction of the ballpark.

"Avery, be careful," said Charlotte, "This telescope is definitely not a toy."

"C'mon," I begged, "let's see."

I hopped up and down, because I was excited about the Red Sox's home field. Charlotte was so fussy sometimes, I mean, what could have happened? How was I supposed to know the board I was hopping on was loose. Just then, the far end lifted like a seesaw, and I dropped like a rock. Thud.

"Whoa." I grunted.

"Are you all right?" asked Charlotte.

She sounded kinda worried. I was fine. I've been through much worse on the soccer field.

"Hey!" hollered Katani. "What's the yo-yo done now? Is everyone all right?"

And there it was. Right next to my face, in a space under the creaky floorboard: a yellowed envelope. I grabbed it and looked inside.

'"What is it?" asked Charlotte.

I held out a parchment paper and a small silver key with sparkling jewels on it.

"You guys!" I hollered. "You're not gonna believe this!"

Charlotte picked up the parchment.

"Wow," she said, softly.

"It's an ancient document or something!" I said.

Charlotte held it carefully, like a newborn baby.

"What's with the excitement, Avery?" called Katani.

"It's a parchment!" answered Charlotte.

"And a key with jewels on it!" I added.

That's the fastest I've ever seen Katani move. Her head popped into the opening.

"Say, what?"

I held up the silver key.

"Those look real!" she whispered. "Bring that down here right now!"

We sat in a circle, passing the key between us. It was small, too small to fit a door. The top was curly, with a sparkly blue stone and a deep red stone attached. Katani held it to the light.

"I think it's a real sapphire and a real ruby."

Charlotte gently unrolled the dried-up paper and studied it.

"Will you look at this!" she whispered. "What do you think *BSG* means?"

"Wow," said Maeve. "It's really serious and old fashioned. 'Never to betray their secrets and sacred trust.' I like that."

"Yeah," agreed Charlotte. "Hey, I think we should have an oath, too."

"Cooool," said Maeve. "A secret meeting place needs a scroll or two."

"What do we want with an oath?" Katani joked, "We don't have to follow tons of rules, do we?"

"No way, Katani," I said. "But, I like Charlotte's idea. Why not update the BSG oath, and really make it ours. It'll be fun. We get to make our own rules."

"Like the Declaration of Independence?" asked Katani.

"Hey," said Maeve, "that's kinda what this one sounds like: 'To hold sacred ... '"

"Sort of," I interrupted. "But it's more like a special BSG Bill of Rights."

"I could get into that," said Katani, "the right to free expression and all."

"Yeah!" said Charlotte. "Next week let's put together our own Bill of Rights."

"Cool," I said.

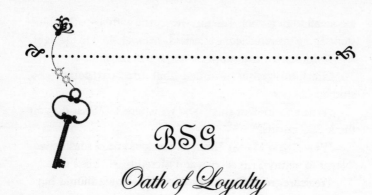

BSG
Oath of Loyalty

*I solemnly swear to be loyal
to the BSG forever.*

*To defend its members
against all manner of evil.*

*Never to betray their secrets and
sacred trust.*

By the order of the

Sapphire and the Ruby

"So, what's the key for?" asked Maeve.

I had totally forgotten!

"Come on!" I said, jumping up. "Let's start looking for the secret doors!"

"Doors!" said Katani. "Avery, this key is too small ... it's for like a box or something."

"Wow! Maybe there's a real treasure hidden somewhere. Let's go!" I said.

We searched every corner of the Tower. Nothing.

"OK!" I said. "Now we spread out and search through the whole house!"

"No!" protested Charlotte in a nervous voice. "We can't."

"Why?" I asked.

"It'll wake up my dad," she said.

"We haven't managed to wake him yet," said Maeve.

"OK," I said. "We won't search the upstairs. We'll just search downstairs."

Charlotte was biting her fingernails like a chipmunk.

"What are you scared of?" I asked.

"Nothing," she said. "I just don't think we should wander around downstairs so late at night."

"Charlotte's right," said Katani. "Why would the key be here if the box isn't? I'll wear the key around my neck 'til then so it doesn't get lost."

"Aw. You just want to wear a jewelry key," I said. "And Charlotte, you're scared of the dark. What about you, Maeve? Are you brave?"

"Sorry, Avery. I've seen too many creepy movies. My parents are running a *Twilight Zone* series this week."

I curled up on the pillows on my window seat and pouted. Charlotte covered me with her comforter.

✿

"I'm sorry," she said, "I'll check downstairs for you as soon as I get the chance."

They debated what the letters B-S-G stood for, until we went to the living room to sleep.

CHAPTER 20

Charlotte

DEEP, DARK SECRETS

I OBVIOUSLY COULDN'T TELL THE GIRLS SATURDAY NIGHT, but I had no intention of poking around downstairs for treasure boxes or secret locks. What if Miss Pierce found me? My lie about owning the Tower House was getting more complicated by the day. I loved having the girls over and pretending the Tower was mine, but I felt like I was living a big lie. I broke a promise to my dad, too. How was I ever going to get out of this? I'd have to figure something out soon.

At lunch, all we talked about were the letters B-S-G. Avery thought it had something to do with Brookline Soccer, but Katani told her that the key was so old there was no way it could have anything to do with soccer.

"When Grandma Ruby was growing up in Brookline, no girl ever touched a soccer ball. She told me if there's one thing she hopes she never sees again in our school, it's dodge ball. That's all they were ever allowed to play here. She hated it."

"Your grandmother went here?" asked Avery.

I remembered Mrs. Fields telling me she had grown up here. I couldn't even imagine anyone being in the same school for that many years.

"Yeah," answered Katani. "It was a high school then, not a junior high. There were only about half as many kids, too. And it was pretty much all white."

"Let me see the key again, Katani," said Avery.

"I don't have it," said Katani.

"Whaddya mean?" shouted Avery.

"You didn't lose it, did you?" Maeve asked, worried.

"Chill," said Katani. "It's in my bureau drawer in my velvet jewelry box where no one can find it."

"I thought you were going to wear it on your chain," I said. "Did it clash with your outfit or something?"

"Worse," said Katani. "Last night, when I went to dinner, I had forgotten to slide the chain inside my shirt, like I've been doing. When Grandma Ruby saw it, she almost dropped a pot of mashed potatoes. She gave me the freakiest look and asked me where I got it, like I had stolen it or something. I told her a friend gave it to me, but I don't think she believed me. She just kept staring and asking questions. We need to keep it hidden."

"Let's just bring it back to its home in the floorboard, then," said an impatient Avery.

"I promise," said Katani. "I'll put it back at our next sleepover."

Before she could answer, Ms. Rodriguez came up behind us. "I hate to interrupt you four while you're discussing deep, dark secrets," she said, "but the bell rang three minutes ago."

While I broke into a silly, guilty grin, Katani managed to stay as cool as ever. "No deep, dark secrets Ms. Rodriguez," she said. "We're just discussing current events."

"Excellent," said Ms. Rodriguez. "I'm sure Mr. Danson will be interested in hearing all you have to share."

As we headed toward history, Katani grumbled, "Ms. R is everywhere. It's like she has super powers or something."

Our history teacher, Mr. Danson, is young and very cool. He's always talking about bands, TV shows, and great restaurants he's been to over the weekend. The only thing I don't like is that he tends to call on kids who *don't* have their hands up. When he asked what the Oregon Trail was, I just knew I should have just raised my hand ... but I didn't ... so of course, he called on me.

"A rock band?" I guessed

Avery and Nick started laughing.

But seriously, how was I supposed to know that? I haven't studied American History in a long time!

THE LIE GROWS

My new friends still didn't understand why the grand piano always had a cover on it or why we never used the downstairs. One day, I heard Katani talking to Avery in the Tower when they thought I was still in my bedroom. "If it were me, I'd eat every meal in the dining room underneath that luxurious chandelier. But Grandma Ruby says writers march to the beat of a different drummer." If being from an odd family of writers was the rumor I needed to cover my lie, that was fine with me.

Every time we came back to the house, it was hard to keep Avery from prowling around looking for the supposed "treasure" downstairs.

"It's no use, Avery. I already looked everywhere," I said. "I'm telling you. The box must have been in the Tower and someone's taken it. Why would a box not be right next to the key? Aren't you late for soccer practice?"

"Yikes," she yelped. "You're right. I'm outta here."

Avery dashed for the front door. Phew! Saved by the bell. I couldn't imagine which would be worse—having to tell my friends I lied or having a landlady kick me and Dad out of the place I was starting to love more than anywhere else in the world. That's the problem with a lie ... you can't relax about things.

To: Sophie
From: Charlotte
Subject: Re: this and that

hi sophie -
i miss you. how is paris? have u been to deux garçons? i miss having a cafe au lait and walking along the Seine. lots is going on here. I have 3 new friends—believe it or not, they're from my lunch group! ... it's a long story. anyway, maybe u can visit at christmas and meet them if they're still around. Who are your friends this year? I'm doing ok in school. science is earth science. can't wait till we do astronomy. math is OK. we're multiplying fractions, something that i learned in 2 other countries so it's easy. when we do percents my friend katani can help me. she's brilliant. nick the boy who always laughs at me is my partner for history. He's really nice and very smart. we have decided to get married. don't panic. just in class. we have to cross the oregon trail together

with our pretend babies. how embarrassing.
that's all I can think of for now. BFFAE.
love,
charlotte

CHAPTER 21

Katani

THE BSG IS CALLED TO ORDER

CHARLOTTE SPENT ALL WEEK talking about the update to the old BSG oath. Avery was pretty excited, too. Ms. R's response to her "other" letter had Avery all fired up.

"What we think really does matter," Avery had said. "We don't think anyone else will care, so we don't even try."

I don't think I've ever had a problem speaking my mind, but not everyone has as cool a grandmother as I do. She taught my mother and all her grandkids that we matter. Having our own Bill of Rights would really be fun.

Saturday we had a fun dinner and hung out with Charlotte's dad while we made s'mores, but the fun really began after he went to bed. We climbed into the Tower and Charlotte began the first official meeting of the new BSG— whatever that stood for.

"Welcome, fellow members of the BSG," she said, "... to our first official meeting. Tonight's agenda:

1. *Assign official titles for BSG members.*
2. *Announce official BSG meeting regulations.*
3. *Write the new BSG Bill of Rights.*

"Avery will be President and run the meetings. I'll be the Keeper of the Records, taking notes at every meeting. Katani will be Chief Personal Problem Solver, in charge of making the lives and looks of her BSG sisters more beautiful."

"I'd like to be Cruise Director!" interrupted Maeve.

"I had you down as Minister of Fun, Romance, and Entertainment," said Charlotte.

"Same thing. But I've always wanted to be called the 'Cruise Director.' It has a lovely ring to it."

"How can you cruise if you're not on a boat?" asked Avery.

"Watch me," said Maeve. She turned and pulled Hawaiian necklaces out of her bag, loaded hula music into her boom box and began to move her hips in a circle. Pretty soon we were all trying to copy her. Except for Maeve, we were pathetic. She must have double jointed hips or something.

Finally Charlotte gasped, "You can have any title you want, Maeve, as long as we don't have to hula anymore."

During a cold cereal break, Charlotte taped this poster on the wall:

❧ .... ❦

OFFICIAL BSG MEETING REGULATIONS

1. *Official food: definitely Brownies!*
2. *Official song: Whatever "Cruise Director" Maeve decides fits the mood of the meeting.*
3. *Agenda: each Saturday's sleepover meeting will be planned one week in advance.*

"So," said Avery, "how about this Bill of Rights?"

"I thought I might as well start as Keeper of Records tonight," said Charlotte. She propped a big pad of newsprint on her desk and folded back the cover to show the heading she'd made:

❧ .... ❦

The New Tower Rules
*Created by The Newest Order
of The Ruby and The Sapphire*

Be it resolved that all girls are created equal ...

"Ready when you are," she said with a big red marker in her hand.

"Oooh, me!" I said. "We, the BSG that is, won't make any rules that stop us from speaking our minds."

"But try not to be too annoying," cracked Maeve.

"I'm not writing down that part," said Charlotte. "But funny, Maeve."

"Why don't you go next, Maeve?" suggested Avery.

"OK," she said. "Something like: We won't put ourselves down if we aren't super-smart, super-coordinated, or a supermodel, because we *always* do the best we can."

"Got it," said Charlotte. "OK, here's one: We'll be loyal to our friends and will trust them, even if they make a mistake or do something totally embarrassing."

"Like getting a tablecloth caught in your zipper in the cafeteria," said Maeve in a loud whisper.

Charlotte blushed.

"It's true," I said. "And we're all here, aren't we? Now, hush up, Maeve, this is good."

"We should just go for it," said Avery, "How will we know what we can do if we don't try? We should stand tall and stay true to our own best selves!"

I couldn't help it. I had to ask. "Girl, did all four-and-a-half feet of you just say 'stand tall'?"

"So much for 'trying not to be annoying,'" snapped Avery.

"I," interrupted Maeve, "thought of another one. I don't think we should hang out with nasty people, you know the type, their initials begin with A and J. People who try to put someone down. They have got to go!"

"Ooooh," I said. "I like that one."

"Me, too," said Avery.

Charlotte was doing her best to keep up. She was also getting red ink all over herself.

"Ready," she said.

Avery went next.

"We should, you know, try and eat some healthy food and be active. I mean, how can you chase your dream if you are a couch potato? Now drop and give me 20, Maeve."

"I don't think so," said Maeve. "I'm resting."

"We can take care of the planet too," said Charlotte.

"And help others that don't have as much," offered Maeve.

"How about: We will dare to be fashion individualistas — like we should be able to wear white socks when we want to," I suggested.

"That doesn't sound as important as some of the other things," said Avery.

"Well, excuse me," I said.

"But it's still good, Katani," replied Avery. "Let's do amendments."

"That's great," said Charlotte. "Anything else?"

"I got one," said Maeve. "It's OK to veg out sometimes — just because we feel like it!"

"And: We should totally have as much fun as we possibly can," said Avery.

Suddenly, I remembered my business plan. "We should try to save money so we'll be able to start a business or buy a house if we want. Dreams are important for girls."

"And unlimited amendments," said Maeve. "So the list can grow. I mean we might think up other important stuff."

"That's a really good one," said Avery.

"Yeah, I think we should put that one first," said Charlotte, her hands a marker-stained mess." Would anyone like to submit suggestions for next week's meeting?"

"Yeah!" said Maeve, giggling. "Quit using fancy words like 'submit.'"

"Well, how about a game of soccer on Saturday?" Avery asked.

Now, why was I not surprised she said that?

"I'll play," said Charlotte. "I was on a team in Australia."

That got our attention.

"I played defense, I was a stopper," she told us.

"Well that totally figures," said Maeve. "Your dancing suggests a violent past."

Avery was excited. I guess I could play. No coaches would be looking over my shoulder and comparing me to Patrice.

And that was it: the end of our first BSG meeting. Charlotte promised to type up The New Tower Rules on cool paper so we could put it under the floorboard by the telescope. We headed downstairs to sleep.

THE NEW TOWER RULES
CREATED BY THE NEWEST ORDER
OF THE RUBY AND THE SAPPHIRE

Be it resolved that all girls are created equal!

1. We will always speak our minds, but we won't be like obnoxious or anything.
2. We won't put ourselves down, even if we aren't super-smart, super-coordinated, or a supermodel.
3. We'll be loyal to our friends and won't lie to them even if they make a mistake or do something totally embarrassing.
4. We will go for it—how will we know what we can do if we don't try?
5. We will try to eat healthy and stay active. How can you chase your dream if you can't keep up?
6. We won't just take from people and the planet. We'll try to give back good things too.

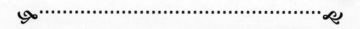

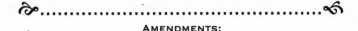

Amendments:

1. We can all add as many amendments as we like.
2. We will dare to be fashion individualistas—like we're all different so why should we dress the same?
3. Sometimes we'll veg out—just because we feel like it!
4. We should try to save money so if we ever want to, we can start a business or something someday.
5. We should have as much fun as we can.

CHAPTER 22

Avery

BAD SPORTS

THE BSG ROCKED. I loved our New Tower Rules. Could we be loyal? Could we be true to each other? Why not? Girls don't always have to be mean to each other. My first personal test was basketball. Even though everyone plays soccer in the fall, Mr. McCarthy, our gym teacher, is completely obsessed with basketball. Rumor has it that he almost went professional. So now, every rainy day, all the gym classes have to play b-ball.

I picked Katani and Charlotte for my team. They looked completely shocked, but if I was going to be loyal to the BSG, I was going to have to follow our rule of trusting them even if they did something embarrassing. (Besides, maybe I could improve their games a little.)

Ever since the first class, Mr. McCarthy had acted like Katani was a big disappointment. He always picked me and Anna as captains. It wasn't much fun being the gym teacher's pet now that I was friends with Katani and knew how rotten Mr. McCarthy made her feel.

Anna picked Joline—big surprise—and Nick. I also had

Maeve and the Trentini twins. Maeve wanted to guard Nick closely. I let her, even though I knew gazing at her favorite hottie would blind her to the basketball. I passed to Charlotte and Katani no matter how many times they dropped it.

We didn't have a chance. Anna and Joline towered over me every time I tried to shoot or drive to the hoop. But, Charlotte grinned every time I passed the ball to her and then passed it right back. I managed to get the ball to the Trentinis a few times, but with only five minutes to go we were losing by eighteen points.

I noticed Ms. Rodriguez had come in and was sitting in the front of the bleachers.

Mr. McCarthy noticed her, too.

"Ms. Rodriguez," he said. "To what do we owe this special pleasure?"

"Well, Mr. McCarthy," she answered, "since it's so early in the school year, even I don't have a lot of homework, so I thought I'd come watch for a few moments."

We got the ball in play again, and I put Katani by the net and gave her plenty of chances to shoot, even though she didn't want them. Mr. McCarthy shook his head every time I passed to her, which made me really mad. Didn't he get it that I was trying to teach her? Because he sure wasn't interested in doing it. I really got into having Katani score a basket.

In the last minute, I stole the ball from Anna, drove down court, and threw a quick pass to Charlotte ... which she caught. Things were looking up. She passed it right back again. So I fired it back to her.

"Dribble three times towards the basket," I hollered.

I thought I saw her lips moving as she counted out three dribbles, but she pulled it off and threw the ball back to me with grateful relief.

Charlotte had bumped into Anna, which cleared the basket. Katani was begging me not to pass it to her, so I headed in for an easy lay-up.

"Ten seconds!" shouted Mr. McCarthy. "Quit foolin' around and take your shot, Short Stuff!"

Short Stuff? Nobody calls me "Short Stuff!"

"Katani," I yelled, as I lobbed the ball toward the backboard. "Tap it in!"

Even if Katani couldn't play basketball, she'd watched her sisters enough to know what I meant. She jumped, took a mid-air swipe at the ball, and—whaddaya know—she tapped it in.

"SCORE!" I yelled running toward her for a high five.

The look on Katani's face was incredible. It made me feel almost as good as if we had won. The look on Mr. McCarthy's face made me feel even better. Ms. Rodriguez, who had come to collect us, was sitting up in the bleachers cheering.

"Mr. McCarthy?" called Katani.

"Yeah, Summers," said Mr. McCarthy gruffly.

"I think we should play five more minutes with the low baskets." Katani continued: "I say we try a five-minute rematch where the taller kids still have to shoot regulation height and the shortest kids shoot into the lower baskets.

"You know—the low rollaway baskets underneath the regulation ones so it's fairer for anyone under five feet?"

Mr. McCarthy's face went red.

I could see Ms. Rodriguez smiling all the way from the other side of the gym.

"We're outta time," growled Mr. McCarthy.

"Nice try," said Anna sarcastically.

"Actually," Ms. Rodriguez called out, "This class is a little farther down the Oregon Trail than the other classes, and Mr. Danson is in a meeting right now. So a few extra minutes more won't hurt."

Mr. McCarthy looked annoyed. We were probably interfering with his coffee break. Too darn bad. The class was so excited, they were already rolling the lower baskets into place. Sammy, the only kid under five feet besides me, looked like he'd won the lottery. For once, he'd have the same chance at a shot as Nick, Anna, and the Trentinis.

"Here are the rules," I shouted, throwing Sammy a pinney and putting on one myself. "Anyone with a pinney shoots at the lower baskets. The rest of you can shoot at regular baskets."

"No fair," said Anna tossing her hair back like she was an actress on TV.

I didn't have to argue back. Team BSG came to my rescue. "For your information," said Katani, walking up to Anna, "there is the same distance between Avery and the top of the shorter basketball hoop and you and the top of the regular one. Maybe even a little less, but that's OK because you'll need every advantage you can get."

"All right, Summers. That's enough," said Mr. McCarthy. "Let's get going. You kids have five minutes to finish this up."

Once we got started, those two witches, Anna and Joline, never passed to Sammy—or anyone else for that matter. Everyone on my team fed it to me. I loved these guys! The hoop was finally within range. Even with Anna guarding me, I crushed a dunk right over her head!

We won! Anna and Joline tried to pretend it wasn't a real game but you could tell they were mad. For Team BSG, it was a major victory! I thanked Katani. So did Ms. Rodriguez.

"That was an interesting way to change the rules," she said as she looked at Katani.

CHAPTER 23

Maeve

RULE #3

MS. RODRIGUEZ WAS NOT THE TYPE TO LET US slide through Monday morning first period on auto pilot. If she noticed the class was dead, which we totally were that day, she'd come up with an idea to shake us awake.

"For your Creative Writing assignment this morning, I would like you to write a story."

Everyone groaned.

"Not your own story ... a class story."

This perked everyone up a little.

"When I call your name, I want you to come to the board and write the most exciting thing you can think of to keep the story going. By the end of class, we should have something good enough to sell to Hollywood. The only rules are: no violence, no TV characters, and no ending with 'Then I woke up. It was all a dream.' Maeve, could you start us off?"

I couldn't believe she was calling me to the board! She knew what a hard time I had spelling. Please don't let me make a fool of myself, I thought, as I walked up there. My stomach was in knots. My palms sweaty. Every kid in the class was staring at me, especially Nick.

"I'm so lonely up here," I giggled, trying to make a funny joke. People laughed. They didn't know that I was actually telling the truth.

"Don't worry, Maeve. You won't be alone long. All you have to do is write the title. With your dramatic skills and sense of story, I thought you'd be perfect for that. Charlotte, why don't you come up, and be ready to write the first sentence."

I absolutely adore Ms. Rodriguez. She had purposely given me the shortest task. I really shouldn't have doubted her for a minute.

I thought for a second. The hero of our story should definitely be a kid. I've seen about a million movies and the ones that really get me are the ones where kids are somehow split from their parents. Ever since I first saw Dumbo's mother locked up and singing to him through the jail bars, those scenes have absolutely killed me. I wrote my title: THE RUNAWAY GRIL.

Out of the corner of my eye, I saw Joline turn to Anna and laugh. What was so funny? To make things worse, Charlotte tripped, nearly knocking me over. The poor kid probably couldn't see with all that hair covering her face. I tried not to be mad that she had messed up my title with her marker. Now it read: THE RUNAWAY GRILL.

"Thank you Maeve," said Ms. Rodriguez. "You may sit down now."

"Cool idea, Maeve," said Charlotte, loud. It wasn't until she began to write her sentence, that I realized I had written "gril" instead of "girl," and that Charlotte had changed my title on purpose, to save me from being the laughingstock of Ms. R's class.

Charlotte read her sentences out loud. "Who would have

❀

thought an innocent family picnic at the top of a hill could cause such destruction? By the time the grill with the loose wheel had rolled through the fireworks factory by the corn field, the entire town was covered with popcorn."

"Nice!" said Nick.

"Some girls should rethink their posture," Anna hissed as Charlotte slunked back to her seat, trying to be invisible.

"Anna," said Ms. Rodriguez, who never missed a thing. "Please come up and continue."

I smiled at Charlotte when she sat down.

"Thanks!" I whispered. "You're the best." I absolutely adore that girl.

CHAPTER 24

Avery

THE NEWEST MEMBER

SATURDAY WAS SOCCER DAY. The BSG had agreed to meet at the field behind school at four, so we could play before dark. I was really surprised when Charlotte showed up in cleats and Katani and Maeve were wearing shoes they could actually play in. This could be fun.

We started passing the ball around. It went well enough, so we tried playing some two on two. It had rained earlier, so it was a little muddy and slippery for Maeve and Katani, but they actually enjoyed playing because no one was yelling at them for doing something wrong.

"This isn't so bad," said Katani. "Maybe my problem is hand-eye coordination."

The trouble was, no one could get past Charlotte, not even me. She was amazing. It was like she said; there was something about her clumsiness that went well with playing defense. I started thinking that maybe she's not really clumsy, but more like "attracted to things." This is bad if it's hot soup, or an open door, but it's great if it's the soccer ball you've just taken away from someone. I started wondering if

✿

Charlotte might want to try out for my travel team.

We ended for the day with some shots on goal. I got in goal and watched Maeve and Katani flail away. Charlotte talked to them about kicking, but that was going to take some time. We were a long way from corner kicks or crosses.

Another wild kick from Maeve sent the ball into the bushes behind the goal. Racing to get there first, Charlotte and I both charged headlong when suddenly, Charlotte tripped over a garbage can that had fallen on its side. She looked so funny, just like an *I Love Lucy* prank. I was about to hoot with laughter. Then I heard it. We both heard it. A high pitched howl coming from the garbage can. Something short and kinda fat ran into the bushes. Charlotte made an "eeeww" face.

"That looks like a big, fat white rat! Let's get out of here," she said, pulling herself up quickly. Unfortunately, she got her feet all tangled together and promptly tripped back over the can again. That set off another yowl, this one louder.

"That's no rat," I said. "It's a ... OMG ..." Something rushed me. Charlotte screamed and grabbed my arm.

"Ohh! It's just a little dog. Charlotte ... you can let go of my arm now," I said.

"I'm sorry. It's just that he looked like some kind of huge mutant rat."

We both stared at the muddy little thing sitting in front of us. He was about as big as the soccer ball and looked like a scruffy little terrier, with one gray ear turned up. Most parts of him were probably white, but he was so dirty you could hardly tell. He was also a little funny looking. But he looked like the kind of dog you wouldn't say that to.

"Do you think he's lost?" asked Charlotte

The little guy cocked his head like he was listening to us.

"I think so. We have leash laws in Brookline; dogs definitely can't be loose in the park. And look at him, he's so dirty. Nobody would let their dog in the house like that."

The little dog barked at us and then promptly sat down in front of my feet.

Charlotte said that she didn't think he liked to be called "dirty." "Dogs have feelings too."

"We can't just leave him here," I said.

"Should we pick him up?" asked Charlotte in the kind of voice that meant, "If we have to, could you do it please?"

"Well, I'm not sure if we really should 'cause we don't know if he has his shots or not," I told her.

The little guy must have been really upset when he heard that because, all of a sudden, he jumped up and did a flip in the air like a circus dog or something.

"OMG," gushed Maeve, who had run over with Katani to see what all the commotion was about. "That's the cutest little thing even if it is completely, disgustingly filthy."

Katani looked a little skeptical. "Do you think that he's a friendly dog?"

That did it.

The little mutt started running in and out of our legs at a zillion miles an hour. Suddenly, he stopped in front of me, stood up on his little hind legs, and seemed to beg for me to pick him up.

Maeve bent down and looked at his collar.

"Avery, he's got a rabies tag hanging off his collar and it says the date on it. I think it's safe to pick him up. Plus, he seems really friendly to me."

That's all I needed to hear. I pulled my sweatshirt off, bent down and wrapped it around him. Boy did he stink ... goodbye sweatshirt. I picked him up, and with a contented little snort, he snuggled deep into my arms. He looked up at me with mischievous, brown doggie eyes that seemed to say, "This works for me." It was love.

"Guys, I know he looks like a drowned, oversized hamster," I said. "But he's a dog. A little lost dog ... an orphan. See? He doesn't even have a nametag on his collar—just the rabies tag. We have to help him."

"Phew!" said Katani holding her nose. "Well, maybe we should give him a bath."

"Let's give him a bath at Charlotte's, she's right across the street!" Maeve offered.

The little guy looked up at me and cocked his ear. Maybe he likes how he smells, I thought.

Charlotte was still wiping stuff from her glasses.

"What?" she said. "We can't bring a dog to my house, especially a dirty, smelly one! He may have fleas. He probably belongs to someone."

"Yeah, someone who abandoned him long enough to get this dirty. And hungry! Hey, I'll bet he's hungry, aren't you, little guy?"

Charlotte grumbled, rubbing a few scratches on her arms.

"This dog needs a home!" I said, looking from one to the other of them.

"My parents won't let us have a dog," said Katani. "They say it's not fair when we barely have time or space for the members of our own family."

"We tried having a dog once," said Maeve, "but he barked every time the previews started, so we had to give him away."

"My Mom's allergic ... So, I guess Charlotte, you're the only one. There's nowhere else. Pleeeeease, Charlotte," I said. "I've wanted a puppy my whole life and I've never been able to have one."

The dog licked my cheek and then stared at Charlotte. I tried to match his pathetic look by sticking out my lower lip. How could she resist us?

"I'm not allowed to have pets," she said. "Otherwise I'd have another cat."

My lip started to tremble. This time I wasn't faking. I was about to cry. We couldn't just leave him here.

"Could we just hide him in the Tower for a few days?" I begged. "You can take his picture with your digital camera, and we'll make a poster. My mother has a friend who was a vet. She'll check him out and then I'll put posters up, and we'll see if an owner wants him back."

"Oh, right, Avery," grumbled Charlotte. "And whose phone number are you going to give them? Not mine."

"I'll make up a special email name, just for this!"

Charlotte sighed. "I know I'm going to regret this. All right, but just for a few days."

"Oh thank you, thank you, thank you!! You're my best friend in the entire world!"

The dog tried to scramble up and lick Charlotte's ear. Good move, dude, I thought. I scooped him up and tucked him into my soccer bag. Then we headed up the hill to Charlotte's house.

DOG IN TUB ... AND EVERYWHERE

We left off our muddy shoes on the front porch. Charlotte's dad had left a note that he was out picking up Chinese food, so I thought it was safe to take the dog out of my soccer bag. As soon as I unzipped the bag, he jumped out and ran up and down the stairs, leaving muddy paw prints everywhere. Charlotte had a fit.

"Catch him! Avery, he cannot be loose in this house!"

"Gotcha!" I said, grabbing him.

"The first thing we need to do is clean him," said Katani. "The smell is killing me. Come with me to Charlotte's bathroom, dog."

"Wait a minute!" said Charlotte. "What about this mess? How do we get the dirt up before Dad gets home?"

"I have an idea," said Maeve.

She ran outside, quickly put on her filthy sneakers, and handed us ours.

"Watch this."

She followed the paw prints up and down the stairs, slapping sneaker prints over every single one. After we joined in, it looked like we had run races from the front door to the second floor.

"Brilliant," I said. "No one will ever know a dog's been here."

"Let's just hurry and get him into my bathroom," said Charlotte, looking nervous.

I held the little dog tight in my arms.

"No more adventures for you until you've had a complete 'Katani Makeover.'"

Katani loaded the tub with bubble bath and lukewarm water. The dog began barking and yipping. As I put him into the tub, he tried to run in mid-air and began to bark for real. Then we heard the front door open. Charlotte's dad was home.

"What's happened downstairs?" he asked. "Were you playing soccer or mud-wrestling?"

The dog let out a bark. Charlotte turned the shower radio on full blast.

"Avery!" she whispered. "Keep him quiet."

"Charlotte! What's that racket?"

"Hi, Dad! Sorry! Must be the song on the radio!" She pulled the bathroom door shut behind her.

"Yeah! 'Who Let the Dogs In,'" said Katani.

We all dissolved in nervous giggles.

"Shhh!" begged Charlotte.

"Anyone want Chinese food?"

"Coming! We're just getting washed up!"

I scrubbed the dog, rinsed him, and he took it pretty well. His collar was really dirty, so I gave it to Maeve to wash in the sink. She held the dirty collar away from her, as if it might be alive.

"Yuck," said Maeve. "Couldn't we just toss this? It's totally disgusting."

"No, Maeve," I answered. "The poor little fella's lost, or worse, abandoned. We've got to save anything that will help us know who the real owner is. We don't even know this dog's name."

"Oh, please," said Maeve. "How hard can it be to name a little dog?"

She handed the collar to Charlotte.

"Well, for your information," I answered, "once it learns a name, a dog won't respond well to anything else."

"Avery," said Charlotte, "you're just making a really big deal about nothing."

Charlotte tossed the collar to Katani.

"Ewwww," said Katani. "Thanks for nothing."

"I mean," Charlotte continued, "how hard could it be to name a dog?"

"Yeah," Katani chimed in. "Just pick any old name."

"Oh, so it's that easy, is it?" I asked.

I was starting to get tired of them not taking this seriously. Fine. I'd show them.

✿

"Go ahead, then," I said. "Pick a name."

"Who me?" asked Katani.

"It's just a dog, Avery," said Charlotte. "How tough could it be?"

"I don't care, if you're all so smart, why don't you all try."

"Oh, well ..." said Maeve.

"How ..." said Charlotte.

"... about ..." said Katani.

"Mr. Wiggle," Maeve said brightly. "He really likes to wiggle about."

Everyone laughed. I said, "That is the worst name I have ever heard for a dog, Maeve. It sounds more like a name for an earthworm."

Maeve insisted that we try it anyway.

I put him on the floor and called him. "Here, Mr. Wiggle, come here Mr. Wiggle."

No response.

"Even if it is his name," Katani said laughing, "I bet he would like a new one 'cause no self-respecting dog would answer to Mr. Wiggle." Even Maeve laughed.

"Charlotte, why don't you get his collar over there? He's all dry now and we can put it back on him." I picked up my new pet and gave him a scratch behind his ear. Suddenly, his back leg started kicking wildly. And the more I scratched, the faster the leg went. Maeve and Katani went into a complete giggle fit and I started to join them.

Charlotte, who had picked up the collar, told us to be quiet.

"My dad will kill me if he finds this dog up here. Here, let me put his collar on."

She had the leather collar in her hand, and typical Charlotte, somehow she dropped it into the soapy, dirty bath. She stuck her hand in to fetch it and than grabbed a towel to dry it off. When she turned it over to dry the back side she let out a yelp.

"Guys, I know his name. Look," she pointed. "It's written on the back of the collar. And then she read out loud, "To our precious little man, Marty, on his fifth birthday."

"Marty," I said loudly to the wiggly bundle in my arm.

"ffwuffwuffwuff!" he barked excitedly.

"Marty," said Charlotte, "Boy, that is kind of a funny name for a dog."

Maeve said she had an Uncle Marty.

Katani thought it sounded like a name an old person would give a dog.

We all grew silent at that one.

"Do you think his owners died?" ventured Maeve.

"Maybe they are in a nursing home and they couldn't keep a dog," Katani followed up with.

I felt sad. I wanted to keep "Marty," but not if some poor old people somewhere were looking for him or thinking about how much they missed him.

"Girls," hollered Charlotte's dad. "Food's getting cold. Is there someone else here?"

"No, Dad," called Charlotte, looking even more nervous than usual.

"Good!" he yelled from the kitchen. "Because, I only got enough food for the four of you. And I thought I heard someone yell 'Marty.'"

"Wurff," answered Marty.

That busted Katani, Maeve, and myself up all over again.

"Shhh!" said Charlotte, looking fiercely at all of us. She opened the door and called, "Party, Dad! Party!"

"Wurff," barked Marty again.

"Hey!" said Charlotte to me, "I thought you said he only

❀

answered to his name."

I shrugged. "Guess he's just Party Marty."

"Woof. Woof."

Even Charlotte was laughing at that point, but we had to cool it or we'd get caught for sure. So, Charlotte and Maeve hustled out to help set up dinner while Katani and I fluffed and dried the most adorable, well maybe most *interesting-looking*, dog in the world. I even let Katani put bows in his fur. I hoped Charlotte wouldn't mind, but I gave Marty a rubber ducky to chew on before we shut him in the bathroom and went to eat. This was definitely the best night of my entire life.

We inhaled wonton soup, dumplings, and Sichuan chicken like vacuum cleaners. All any of us could think about was hiding Marty in the Tower.

"Whoa!" said Charlotte's dad. "Breathe, girls, breathe."

"Sorry, Mr. Ramsey," I said. "We're full already. Could we please be excused?"

"Not so fast," he said. "You ladies appear to have some floor-mopping to think about. But first, I want to hear everyone's fortune."

"Absolutely," said Maeve. "We do that at my house too."

I waited impatiently while everyone read theirs. I've always thought fortune cookies were as dumb as horoscopes and weather forecasts. They make them so vague they fit anybody. But when I read mine, I almost fell off my chair. Lucky I was last, because everyone ran from the table so they wouldn't burst out laughing. My fortune said: "*Look for friends in unexpected places.*" Can you even believe that? This dog was definitely meant for me.

CHAPTER 25

Maeve

THE LOVE DOCTOR

SATURDAY WAS ONLY A FEW DAYS AWAY and I couldn't wait. I wanted to see Marty again. I also planned to show the girls what true romance was all about. Avery had no clue. She figured Nick Montoya was only good for basketball. Katani needed a few tips, too. As gorgeous as she is and even with older sisters, Katani has never been on a date. She says having a grandmother who's a principal stops a lot of boys from coming over to their house—no matter how nice Mrs. Fields is.

Charlotte is, well, Charlotte. She's ... different. You want to know how different? Just check out my conversation with her.

MAEVE: I don't know what to do. Tons of girls want to go out with Nick, Charlotte.
CHARLOTTE: They do? Why?
MAEVE: Cause he's ... I don't know ... really cute ... and he's ... I don't know! He's just great!

CHARLOTTE: So can you please just ask him to do something?

MAEVE: Of course not! Are you crazy? Would Scarlett O'Hara do that?

CHARLOTTE: I don't know. But if you like him—

MAEVE: OMG of course I like him. But it's all strategy. You've got to ... you know ... drop hints first. Then you sorta let him know by accident that you like him. Like you tell his friends or something, or you I.M. someone and they I.M. someone else and he finds out about it. You just can't ask someone out. Never!

CHARLOTTE: OK, Maeve. You're the expert. But it sounds like a long way around to me.

MAEVE: Well, maybe it's 'cause you lived in Europe or something. But, trust me. This is the way it's done.

ଔ

Guess what? My Dad just showed me the film schedule for the week and *Gone With the Wind* is showing Saturday night. This is like destiny. Maybe Charlotte is right—maybe I should just ask Nick out. My way, of course—with a little strategy mixed in. I could see Nick and me and Rhett and Scarlett, and Atlanta burning. It was too romantic for words.

CHAPTER 26

Maeve

RECIPE FOR ROMANCE

"WATCH AND LEARN," I'd told the girls. So, I already had Charlotte's telescope positioned at the table for two in Montoya's window. Her dad was going to be out late at some poetry slam his students had entered. Destiny again! The girls could study my moves at the bakery from afar, and then follow us along our path to the movies. After that, they'd just have to wait for me to get back to the Tower for all the juicy details.

In the meantime, Katani decided that I should wear my hair up. She brought along some pictures from *Seventeen* magazine to show me. I couldn't decide between the Audrey Hepburn look or the "Britney" ponytailed look with sparkly pins. It was Avery who said that I should wear the ponytail. She said that since I did not have a cigarette holder, big sunglasses, and a black dress, my hair might look a little over the top in my blue jeans. She had a point.

We went with the ponytail. Katani said she'd done this look on Kelley plenty of times, so it was no problem. She got out her brushes and combs and pins and went to work. I felt like a goddess in some fancy Hollywood salon. Although at one point I did have to tell Katani not to pull my hair so tight 'cause I felt my face was being pulled back like I had been in a wind tunnel or something. She told me to "just relax," adding "no pain, no gain" as she stuck a sparkly pin into my scalp.

Charlotte decided that I absolutely had to have nail polish to complete the look. She thought a bright color with little white hearts would be perfect. So did I. As she knelt beside me painstakingly painting hearts on top of "Glamour Girl Pink" polish, Marty decided to give me his own pedicure. He licked my toes until I couldn't stand it any more. It tickled so bad I made Avery put him on his bed. She gave him a piece of a cracker so he would stay. Avery, to all our amazement, went through all of Charlotte's potions and lotions to find the perfect fragrance for me. She decided on "Gardenia Love Potion." "Maeve, if this doesn't do the trick, I don't know what will," she sneezed. "You're gonna smell like a flower garden in spring. What boy wouldn't love that?" My confidence was soaring by the moment.

I sat there in the "Lime Swivel" as everyone put on the final touches. Katani told Avery to lighten up on the perfume or "Nick might get sick and throw up" after Avery sprayed my whole head with it. Avery got a little mad, but I told her that her choice was perfect and that I felt like a princess. She was happy about that.

Finally, Katani held up a mirror for me to see. I don't mean to sound vain or anything, but my hair looked so adorable it almost took my own breath away. I told Katani that she was a "Style Miracle Worker." She beamed. When Charlotte added that I looked so good it couldn't help but be a perfect evening, I had to give her a hug.

I told them all that they were the best friends any girl could have.

It was time to go. Katani reminded me to walk with my theme song, "It's Raining Men," in mind. Then I handed out cards to the BSG and told them to pay careful attention.

Romantic Evening Recipe Card

Ingredients:

1 Romantic Boy (if too hard to find, substitute
1 unsuspecting boy)
1 Romantic Girl
1 Frozen Hot Chocolate, Maeve style
2 Straws
2 Free Movie Tickets (easier if you don't mention
it's a romantic movie)

Directions:

Invite boy to help you with homework at Montoya's Bakery. Say that you couldn't possibly drink a whole frozen hot chocolate but that you would love the teeniest sip of one. Immediately upon delivery, stick two straws in drink. When he dips to drink, do same. If he tires of this, finish frozen hot chocolate yourself (win/win situation).

Casually wave movie tickets. When he looks interested, say you must do your homework first. After a few minutes, mention how cool it is to own a movie theater and be able to eat all the popcorn and Slushies you want for free. When he looks interested, say you need to do more homework. After five more minutes of homework, look at your watch, and say, "Gosh, the seven o'clock show

*is about to start. Would you like to come and we can do
our homework afterwards?"*

*Sit in private balcony box of Beacon Street Movie
House. Watch movie. Prepare for romance!*

ℭℛ

Sitting in Montoya's with Nick, it was all I could do not
to look up at the telescope and wink. I grabbed two straws.
Steering him to the table was no problem, but the double
straw thing turned out to be harder than I thought.

"So what homework do you need help on?" he asked.

"Umm ... I bet you're thirsty ... You've been working so
hard," I said.

"Not really," he said. "I'm good. So what do you need
my help on?"

"Look—this iced hot chocolate is huge. Let's share it. I
insist," I said.

"OK," Nick said, giving me a weird look. "When are we
getting to the homework?"

I tried looking up at him like Audrey Hepburn in *Sabrina*,
but when Nick went in for a sip, our heads bumped. Hard.

"Ow!" he said.

"Oops!" I must have turned as pink as my straw. "You
go." I offered.

He leaned down to his straw again. Now was my chance.
I leaned forward and tried to brush his cheek with mine.

"Maeve," said Nick. "Your hair's in the hot chocolate.
Why don't you have the rest?"

Not exactly the romantic warmup I planned. Oh well.
Nevermind. I slid my chair to Nick's side of the table and
pulled out my favorite notebook—the one with the purple
stripes and green zigzags.

"I need help with math," I said, opening my notebook between us, nice and cozy. "Could you show me how to multiply the denominators on this one?"

Nick slid his chair an inch to the right. Hey! Where was he going?

"Sorry, I'm left-handed," he explained. "I can't write when you're that close."

"You're a lefty!" I exclaimed, inching my chair an inch to the right. "Me too." I made it sound like we were the same astrology sign.

The more Nick explained about denominators, the cuter he looked.

"Maeve, are you getting this?"

"Uh ... sure," I said. "You're a huge help, Nick. And you know what? You've helped me so much that I think we can make the next showing of the movie at the Movie House. Did you know that my mom and dad own it? So, we—uh, I mean I—can go for free whenever we want."

Whew! That was a lot to get out in one breath, but we were running out of time. Nick kept multiplying the stupid fractions. I started stuffing my notebook away.

"Plus the popcorn is great," I added

"Did you figure this problem out yet?" he said.

"Nooo ..." I said in my most patient, understanding voice. "But you know Nick, I think maybe math can wait. But the thing about the movies is ... they kind of start when they start. You know what I mean?"

Nick look confused.

"I thought you wanted to do homework."

"I did! I mean, I do." I fumbled. "There's plenty time for that after the movies."

"Uh ... I'm not sure, Maeve. I'm kinda busy," he said.

I grabbed his arm and pulled him up from the table.

"Please," I begged. "My favorite movie of all time is on!"

I practically had to drag him out of the bakery. But I was sure he'd get into it once he saw the marquee. And he did ...

"Spiderman!" he exclaimed when he saw the marquee. "Awesome! You didn't tell me *Spiderman* was playing. I am a total Marvel Comics freak. I collect any old comics I can get my hands on. I love this movie. I've seen it five times already."

This was not going well.

I had to think fast.

"Oh, you'd be bored stiff, then, seeing it a sixth time. You'll really like *Gone With the Wind*."

Nick hesitated. "Isn't that kind of old? And kind of long?"

"It's ..." I searched for a good answer. "Technicolor! And it's great history. You should see Atlanta burning. Buildings in flames ... dead people everywhere!"

Nick didn't look too sure.

"If you don't like it, you can switch to *Spiderman*," I promised him and grabbed his arm. "You're my guest."

My little brother, Sam, was working behind the counter. I had paid him five bucks in advance to keep quiet when Nick and I got to the theater, and for once Sam earned his pay.

"Who was the kid that got you the popcorn?" asked Nick.

"What kid?" I said.

"The one in camouflage clothes who saluted you when he handed you the popcorn."

"Nevermind," I said in a hurry. "Showtime. You're gonna love the movie."

And then, at long last, we were sitting in the balcony and the movie was about to begin. I sighed with relief. Sharing a bucket of popcorn with Nick Montoya in the balcony of a theater showing *Gone With the Wind*. What could be more romantic? I tried to shift over a little so our knees would touch.

"When's the fire?" whispered Nick.

"In a little while," I said patting his hand. Nick yawned, but I figured he was just a little tired from working at the bakery.

Scarlett and Rhett Butler were about to kiss! My heart started pounding.

"Is it soon?" whispered Nick.

How did he know that the kiss was coming? I couldn't believe we were so in sync. This was it! It was really going to happen.

Just then Atlanta went up in flames.

"All right!" an excited Nick exclaimed. "Now, Maeve, can we go to *Spiderman*?"

It was absolutely the most depressing moment of my life.

Two hours with Katani and half a bottle of hair gel down the drain.

That's when it hit me. True romance is wasted on seventh-grade boys. But, after all, I am an actress in training. I know how to keep my composure.

I stood up and stepped over him.

"Go ahead," I told him flipping back my hair. "Frankly, I don't give a damn.'"

That's my favorite line from *Gone With the Wind* and I've always wanted to use it. At least the evening wasn't a total waste.

CHAPTER 27

Charlotte

THE NORTH STAR

AVERY SAT CROSS-LEGGED WITH MARTY IN HER LAP while I looked through the telescope. "Did you know there's a star named after Marty?" I asked.

"Where?" said Avery moving closer. "Show us."

"Right there," I said aiming the telescope. "Look for the brightest one. It's Sirius, the dog star."

Avery held Marty up to the eyepiece. "Bark if you see the dog star, Marty." Marty didn't bark but he did manage to paw the telescope out of position.

"Hey!" said Avery pushing it back up. "Isn't that Maeve coming up the hill? I thought she said the movie was three hours long!"

I focused the telescope.

"Oh no."

"What's the matter?" called Katani.

"Maeve looks like she's crying," I said.

"Oh dear," said Katani. "I was afraid of that. Avery, don't say a word when she comes up here. You let her do the talking. Our job is to listen."

We scurried about, just to look casual. By the time she opened the trap doors, we were all sitting at our window seats pretending to look busy. Her up-do was more of a down-drop. Long strands of red hair hung around her tear-stained face, making her look even more dragged down and sad.

She took one look at Avery with the dog on her lap, pretending to read it a book, and said, "Nice try. Thanks for not asking, but it was absolutely horrible."

Then she began to blubber. Katani led her to the Lime Swivel, sat her down, and handed her a box of Kleenex. Maeve honked her way through five tissues before speaking.

I brought over a chocolate bar from my stash.

"Oh, I couldn't possibly eat at a time like this," she said, pulling back the wrapper and swallowing a huge piece.

"You don't have to talk about it, if you don't want to," I said politely.

Avery glared at me. She wanted to hear every detail.

Maeve took another bite of chocolate and began her sad tale. "When it comes to romance, seventh-grade boys are hopeless. Consider the time and money wasted," she explained. "Three trips to CVS, twenty dollars on lip gloss, blush, mouthwash, deodorant, and perfume. Six hours of shopping for the right outfit. Add four days and nights rehearsing my lines and moves. What a TOTAL waste!"

"Let's all go down to my bedroom," I suggested. "We need to get out of the Tower. Dad will be home soon."

We sat out on the balcony, on that cool September night. Orion's Belt and the North Star shone clear even with the glow of the city lights.

"It's beautiful!" said Maeve. "A perfect Juliet balcony! 'Romeo, Romeo, wherefore art thou, Romeo?'"

I could tell Maeve was getting back to her old self. She

✿

was over Nick and had moved on to Romeo.

"Brrrr!" said Katani. "It's freezing!"

Avery helped me drag blankets to the balcony. I gave Maeve my special fleece.

"It's so soft!" said Maeve. "Thanks, Charlotte."

Wrapped in blankets, looking up at the stars, none of us spoke for a minute.

"What's that one, Charlotte?" asked Maeve, pointing toward the horizon.

"The North Star. It's always in the same place. It's so steady sailors guide their ships by it."

"Like true friendship," said Maeve.

"Like our friendship," said Katani.

"Thanks for being here," said Maeve.

"No extra charge," said Avery.

"No prob," said Katani.

"Thanks for the cozy blanket, Charlotte."

"I'm just glad you're feeling better, Maeve. We're not used to seeing you sad."

"You're absolutely right," she said. "I gotta snap out of it." She stood up, pulling the blanket around her like a robe. She cleared her throat and sang in a fake opera voice:

"Blankets and stars are the best.
With Nick I was obsessed.
Now I'm feeling better and
I don't need a sweater."

"There's that Miss Piggy influence I was talking about," said Avery.

"Seriously, girls," she said. "What would I do without you? What do kids do who don't have friends?"

"I'll tell you what they do," I said. "They wrap up in blankets and look at the stars by themselves."

"But what if they don't have blankets to wrap up in?"

"What do you mean?" said Katani.

"I mean what if a kid is sick, or poor, or homeless, or in trouble?" Maeve paced the balcony gesturing dramatically with one arm, while holding the blanket around herself with the other. Katani and Avery rolled their eyes. "I mean it," she said. "Without my BSGs and a warm blanket, I know I'd be really sad. How many kids are homeless or friendless or blanket-less tonight? Her voice built to a dramatic crescendo until she shouted to the sky, "EVERY KID IN THIS CITY DESERVES A WARM BLANKET!"

Even though we giggled at her dramatic speech, deep down we knew she was right. I thought about Ms. Rodriguez teaching us to change the rules for people and about Mrs. Fields working to follow her Miss Rumphius quote to make the world a more beautiful place. "What should we do?" I asked.

"So glad you asked," said Maeve looking dreamily into the distance. "We, the BSG, are going to blanket the city with love."

"Hey girls," called Dad from the hall. "I'm back! Who wants to eat?"

ଓ୪

As soon as he went to bed, we snuck back into the Tower. I wished I didn't have to keep secrets from him. Maeve seemed to be recovering nicely from her date and was busy directing activities. "OK, everybody," she said. "It's time to PARTAY WITH MARTAY."

Marty jumped into her arms and licked her face. "That's

my party guy," she laughed. "Get ready for Maeve's dancing lessons!" Marty leapt from her arms and hid behind Avery.

"Yuck," said Avery. "Do we have to?"

Marty trembled and whined.

Maeve ignored both of them. She put on the soundtrack of *Grease*. "Now move everybody, move!"

One look at our moves and she had to catch her breath. After a half hour of frustration, when we were about to give up, Maeve had a great idea. She turned off the music and imitated her reading tutor.

"There's nothing wrong with you. We just have to break the code to your individual learning style. Everyone learns in different ways. You may be pathetic students, but you're all 'special.'"

She took a piece of chalk from my writing supply bag and drew arrows and numbers on the floor. When she finished, we had a complete roadmap for a simple line dance.

"What's this exclamation point?" Avery asked.

"Every time you get to that place in the circle, Marty needs to run through your legs."

"Woof!"

"Awesome!" said Avery.

Maeve's mapping did the trick. By the third time through, even Marty had his part mastered. "We're ready to go on tour!" said Maeve excitedly.

"Sorry, everybody," I said. "This tour's next stop is my bedroom. Time to close up for the night."

"Aw," said Avery. "Do we have to?" Marty jumped into her arms.

"'Fraid so, Avery. Even without shoes, we're making a lot of noise."

"But I thought you said your dad slept through an

elephant stampede," she said, cuddling Marty.

"The elephants sounded like they were on tiptoe compared to you and Katani," I said, shutting off the light.

THE BEST PART

When we finally curled up in our sleeping bags downstairs, Maeve sighed and asked, "Do you think dating ever gets easier?"

"Nah," said Katani. "The good news is, it doesn't matter."

"What do you mean?" asked Maeve.

"Well," said Katani. "I've watched my sisters before and after dates and I've decided the whole thing is a lot like trick or treating."

"Are we going trick or treating together this year, or are we too old?" yawned Avery.

"Go to sleep, Avery," said Maeve. "Keep talking, Katani."

"Collecting the candy is OK, but the dressing up before and the dumping the candy out on the floor and comparing it with your friends afterwards is the best part. You get what I'm saying?"

"I think so," said Maeve.

"The point is my sisters always have a lot more laughs staying up late comparing their dating horror stories than they do on the actual date. And girls always have more fun getting dressed up together than boys will ever know."

I was impressed. I didn't know any of that stuff. Katani definitely has a future in the advice and attitude business. And Maeve seemed satisfied, too.

Katani fell asleep, and Marty and Avery were happily snoring within five minutes.

As I was about to fall asleep, I heard, "Charlotte?"

"Yeah, Maeve?"

"Could we look at the stars one last time?"

"Sure."

We traipsed out to the balcony with our sleeping bags wrapped around us.

"You're like the North Star," she said. "Steady and quiet. You're always there for everyone."

The lump in my throat was so big I couldn't speak. It was the nicest thing anyone's ever said to me.

"Charlotte?"

"Yeah?"

"Mind if I wish on it for Billy Trentini to notice me?"

"No, Maeve."

CHAPTER 28

Katani

TOWER POWER

WHEN MS. RODRIGUEZ ASKED US TO WRITE about our favorite place in our journals, Maeve, Avery, Charlotte, and I all looked at each other and smiled. At lunch time, we read each other's.

At Home in The Tower
A Poem by Charlotte Ramsey

It's a home of my own.
It's a view from the top.
It's a place where the laughing and talking don't stop.
It's the view of my town. It's a view into space—
Books, journals, friends, stargazing—all in one place.
The best thing about having good friends in my home ...
I'm never unhappy. I'm never alone.

My Favorite Place
Avery Madden

Easy. Tower room—Charlotte's house. Why? My dog is there. My friends are there. My older brothers are not there. I can see the lights of Fenway. If I get bored, Katani experiments on my hair, Maeve teaches me dances, and Charlotte shows me the book she's writing about our adventures ... starring ME! (everybody else too.). Best of all, I can curl up with Marty and tickle his tummy.

```
Top Ten Things I Can Do In The Tower
I Can't Do At Home
By Maeve Kaplan-Taylor
```

10. Tape magazine pictures of hotties on the wall.
 9. Talk to my friends in privacy.
 8. Get a snack without Mom studying the fat content on the package.
 7. Go to the bathroom without Sam jumping from the shower stall in combat fatigues.
 6. Look at apartment buildings through the telescope.
 5. Get homework help from "the girls."
 4. Entertain three best friends and a dog from my own, private mini-stage.
 3. Get amazing manicure from Katani, while we dish about Billy. (Nick is off my list.)

2. Paint my wall and windowsill bright pink (or anything that's not "tasteful").

1. Lie around and do absolutely nothing.

My Favorite Place
Katani Summers

You can't understand what the Tower means to me because you've never lived with my sisters. When Candice left for college, Patrice had their whole room to herself. It was so unfair and I still had to share with Kelley. Mom said Patrice had a lot of pressure and needed to keep her grades up for college. Then Patrice "the creep" said Junior High was stupid and doesn't count and Mom got mad but she still wouldn't change her mind.

She says I do the best with Kelley of anyone in the family, which I have to admit is true. I love Kelley. But, sometimes I just need space. That's why the Tower saved my life. For the first time, I can leave my nail polish out without worrying what Kelley might do to it. I can listen to the radio without Kelley covering her ears and yelling. Best of all, I can give my friends advice and makeover tips I learned from my sisters and grandmother, and my friends think I'm really, really smart.

ଔ

PART THREE

BSG: FOR WORSE OR FOR BETTER

CHAPTER 29

Charlotte

CAUGHT

I SHOULD HAVE KNOWN IT COULDN'T LAST. How did I think I could hide four girls and a dog in this house? The truth is, you can trick yourself into believing anything if you want it badly enough, and I wanted the Tower to be for the "BSG" (whatever that meant!) more than I have ever wanted anything. I had never shared so many secrets or laughs as during those Saturday sleepovers. I didn't want it to ever end.

I had overslept because of stargazing too late the night before. To save some time, I left the Tower stairs down when I took Marty out. He was friskier than usual, and I couldn't blame him. The crisp October air quickened our walk. I couldn't believe how beautiful the trees were as the mist lifted over the park. The whole hilltop was on fire with fall color. New England was turning out to be just like I'd imagined when we moved here. I wanted it to last forever. I wanted Brookline to last forever.

I was startled out of my thoughts by a voice.

"Hi, Charlotte. I didn't know you had a dog."

"Nick! What dog? I don't have a dog."

Nick raised an eyebrow. What was he doing here?

"I mean, he's not mine," I mumbled, blushing.

"Where did he come from?"

"Where did *you* come from?"

Nick looked like he was about to laugh. "All right," he said, "I'll go first. I was jogging to the bakery. Dad drives my stuff and I get in some hill running for soccer. Your turn. Whose dog?"

"You wouldn't believe me if I told you," I said.

"I might," said Nick. "Remember, I've heard you call 'The Oregon Trail' a rock band—which would be a great name for a band, by the way—and I've seen you clear a table in seconds. You're pretty funny Charlotte." Then he leaned in toward my face. His lips were so close, like he was actually going to kiss me. I could feel my cheeks turning bright red. This was Maeve's department, not mine.

I yanked Marty and turned to walk away.

"Wait! I meant that as a compliment! Funny is good!"

"We have to go," I mumbled, really embarrassed.

◌Ω

I didn't realize how late I was until I reached the house and could already hear National Public Radio blaring from the second floor. Darn Nick! Darn this dog! I stuck him in my backpack.

"Charlotte!" Dad was shouting from the bedroom window. He never shouts. "Where are you? Are you responsible for these stairs? You haven't been up to the third floor, have you?"

I told myself not to panic. Maybe I could get upstairs and close the trap door before Dad looked at the Tower. But what about Marty? I took a deep breath. Avery and I had prepared for this. I ran out of range of the window and reached into my backpack for the emergency doll clothes I had borrowed from Katani.

"This is for your own good," I said, holding Marty between my knees while I tied the nightcap around his chin.

The dress was tough. Every time I tried to pull his paws through the sleeves, he rolled in my arms.

"Come on, Marty! It's for your own good. You don't want us to get kicked out of the house, do you?"

His brown eyes went all liquidy as he stared up at me. Suddenly, I heard a creak from the back of the house, then a faint laugh. I suddenly remembered the day I called "Hello" to the empty house, and thought I heard an answer. The hair on Marty's back rose as fast as the goosebumps on my arm and he growled when I yanked his paws through the sleeves and spun around.

"Who's there?"

My voice was caught in my throat.

"What do you mean, who's there?" said Dad at the front door in his pajamas. "When were you going to tell me about those stairs? I thought we'd agreed 'no exploring' until we spoke to Miss Pierce. Charlotte, you're in trouble."

He noticed Marty cradled in my arms.

"What in the world is that? I thought you stopped playing with dolls five years ago!"

"It's for school!" I blurted, while I rocked Marty in my arms like a baby.

Dad grunted.

"We'll talk about this later," he grumbled, and went inside. Whew! All I had to do now was get Marty into the Tower. I stuffed him into the duffel, until only his nightcapped head stuck out.

I tiptoed up the front stairs and past the kitchen. Unfortunately, Dad picked that instant to appear in the kitchen doorway with a plate of sizzling bacon.

"Would you like some breakfast?" he asked.

Who knew a small dog wearing a dress could jump out of a backpack? Shock couldn't begin to describe the look on Dad's face as Marty charged into the living room with a piece of bacon hanging from his mouth, and of course, wearing a dress.

"What the heck?"

He chased Marty through the hall only to see him bound up the Tower stairs.

As Dad headed for the steps, I cried, "No, Dad! Please don't go up there!"

"CHARLOTTE ELIZABETH RAMSEY! WHAT IS GOING ON?"

CHAPTER 30

Charlotte

THE TOWER FALLS

I NEVER BROKE MY PROMISE TO THE BSG and our new Tower Rules. I told Dad about my friends and discovering the Tower and finding Marty, but I kept our meetings and our Bill of Rights a forever secret. After seeing what a mess I was over the whole thing as we talked in the living room, Dad agreed not to come upstairs until we had cleaned everything out. But he only gave me two days.

"I'll respect your privacy, Charlotte, but everything has to be out by Saturday night, or I'm going up there. The dog goes to the shelter as soon as I get home from work today.

"Wait," he remembered. "I have meetings this afternoon. And tomorrow. Just great. The dog will have to go to the shelter on Saturday.

"I just don't understand you, Charlotte. You say you love this house and you love living in Brookline. Yet you're willing to risk it all by breaking the only rules we've got. One—don't enter a part of the house that doesn't belong to us without permission from Miss Pierce. And, we haven't even met her yet! Sliding panels and telescoping ladders ought to tell you that that Tower was private. Two—No Pets. What were you thinking?"

Where could I even start?

"I'm disappointed in you. We've never kept secrets from each other. Why now? Help me out here."

I picked at the arm of the living room chair. How could I explain? Dad was right. Honesty was a major thing for me. I don't know how it happened.... Suddenly, I was in deep trouble. I lied to Dad about Marty, and I lied to my friends about the Tower. For the first time in my life the price of not having friends was higher than the price of not sharing everything with him.

"I'm sorry," I said softly. "I'm really sorry, Dad."

He just had no idea how sorry I really was.

☙

I couldn't face telling the girls in person. Every time I rehearsed, I pictured Avery in tears when I told her about Marty going to the shelter on Saturday. I pictured Katani, furious about losing her business headquarters, and Maeve carrying her costumes and stereo away in an absolute huff!

The thought of telling them I'd lied about the house was too much. In the end, I did what I always do when I can't face up to things: I wrote. I couldn't tell them in person. For once, writing was agony for me. I knew it was cowardly. But, I couldn't tell them face to face.

To: Kgirl, flikchic, 4kicks
From: Charlotte
Subject: I'm so sorry

i really don't know how to tell u all
this in person so here I go via email.
the Tower was never mine to share. i
wanted to share it with u so bad after
avery found the stairs that i pretended
it was mine. i pretended so hard even i
started to believe it. the truth is my
dad and i dont own the house. We're only
allowed on the second floor. the lady who
lives downstairs owns it and she doesnt
allow pets.
dad is taking marty to an animal shelter
saturday morning. u have to come get your
things saturday. i hope u don't hate me.
your friend forever even if u do hate me,
charlotte

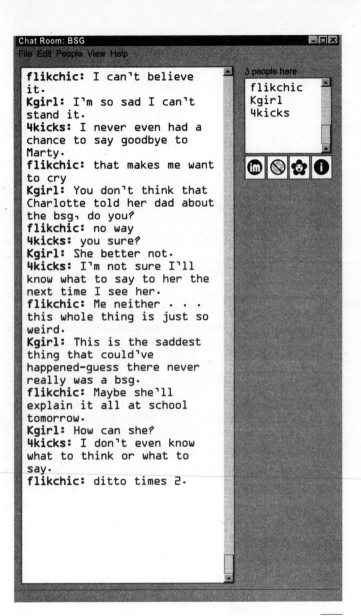

Chat Room: BSG

File Edit People View Help

3 people here

flikchic
Kgirl
4kicks

flikchic: I can't believe it.
Kgirl: I'm so sad I can't stand it.
4kicks: I never even had a chance to say goodbye to Marty.
flikchic: that makes me want to cry
Kgirl: You don't think that Charlotte told her dad about the bsg, do you?
flikchic: no way
4kicks: you sure?
Kgirl: She better not.
4kicks: I'm not sure I'll know what to say to her the next time I see her.
flikchic: Me neither · · · this whole thing is just so weird.
Kgirl: This is the saddest thing that could've happened-guess there never really was a bsg.
flikchic: Maybe she'll explain it all at school tomorrow.
Kgirl: How can she?
4kicks: I don't even know what to think or what to say.
flikchic: ditto times 2.

CHAPTER 31

Charlotte

NOT ABOUT THE DOG

I ALWAYS THOUGHT LUNCH THE FIRST DAY at a new school is the worst. It's not. Lunch when you've made best friends and they won't talk to you is much worse. I bumped into Maeve at our lockers, and she turned bright red and started stammering. I just stared at her. I didn't know what to say. And the next thing I knew, she had twirled her lock combination shut and backed away, looking miserable. I bet she hates me. They all must. I don't even blame them.

At lunch, I didn't even wait to see if they saved my old seat. I was too upset ... and I felt too bad. I took my tray outside; it was cold and windy. A blank, white sky had replaced the gorgeous blue one. I didn't care. I carried my tray to the daycare playground and watched the little kids on the swings. They looked like they didn't have a care in the world. I felt like I'd do anything to be five or six again.

I saw Katani and Avery deep in conversation across the playground, and my stomach felt queasy. Were they talking about me? I hung my head, tears pricking behind my eyelids.

"Hi Charlotte!" came an enthusiastic voice from the

swings. "Are you my new best friend?"

It was Kelley. Kelley on the swings. The one person who liked me no matter what. I set down my lunch, and went over to her. We didn't talk. Kelley sang while we swung. Back and forth. Up and down; it felt good to be like a little kid again and not to think.

Ms. Mathers was watching from the edge of the playground, chatting with Mrs. Fields. When the bell rang, she called, "Time to go, Kelley."

"I don't wanna go!" said Kelley, pumping harder. "I wanna stay outside with my new best friend Charlotte."

I knew exactly how she felt. Having to face those girls in class was weighing on me like a ton of bricks. It was much easier to be with someone like Kelley. Right now everybody else was too complicated.

Mrs. Fields sent Ms. Mathers back to the classroom and came out to the swings to get Kelley herself.

"It's all right, Kelley," I said, slowing down. "We can do this again." My voice wobbled. Like when, I thought?

"It's all right," echoed Kelley, trying to convince herself.

When the swing stopped, she walked over and gave me a big hug.

"I love you, Charlotte."

I had managed to keep myself together the whole time Dad was telling me how disappointed he was in me. And even when I saw my friends—my *old* friends, I held it together. But when Kelley hugged me, I just cried and cried. Then Kelley started crying, too. Mrs. Fields told me to wait on the swings while she brought Kelley back to class.

I broke down and told Mrs. Fields everything. How I had lied to the girls about the whole house being mine, how I'd snuck into the Tower. Even about Marty. As always, she acted as though there was nothing else on her schedule, and I was the only person in the world that mattered. When I told her we were meeting at the house Saturday to clear everything out, she said, "You know, Charlotte, I may just be able to take care of this." I was confused. What could a principal possibly do to help?

◌ℜ

When I got home after school, the house was empty. Really empty. "*Better get used to it,*" I figured.

I took Marty out for a walk. He had spent most afternoons going to the field to practice soccer with Avery, so he dragged me in that direction. I let myself be pulled along and even though it's downhill most of the way, it surprised me how quickly he got us there. I found a stick and threw it to him for awhile, but Marty could tell something was wrong.

He came over and sat, cocking his head. It looked like he wanted me to explain what was going on. Or maybe he was wondering where Avery was, if she would come. I know that's what I was wondering. I missed Avery. I missed taking shots on her in goal. I've always been a good student, but because of Avery, for once in my life, I'd felt like I was good at sports too. And that I even like them.

It was getting late, but I was stalling going back to the house. Nick would be at soccer practice by now, so I just walked past Montoya's, even though Marty was interested in the smells. Maybe Yuri would cheer me up, I thought, but he had a line of customers that went out the door. I crossed Harvard Street. Then I saw Avery coming my way, her duffel slung over one shoulder.

"Hey," I said, as Avery stooped so Marty could jump into her arms. He gave her doggy kisses and wiggled.

"Hi," answered Avery. She looked embarrassed and cleared her throat.

"I'm really, really sorry about Marty."

"Poor Marty," she murmured. "So I guess it's the shelter, after all." She scratched behind his ears.

"What do you say, pal? Wanna make a break for it?" She held him in front of her, looked into his doggy eyes, and hugged him.

"What do you want, Marty?" she whispered. "Huh, boy?"

"Wurff."

"Me, too."

Then she closed her eyes and lowered him to the ground.

"Well ... I guess I better go. I'm late," she said, chewing on her lip.

"Do you want to come see Marty tonight?" I asked.

"I don't think so, Charlotte." She wouldn't even look at me.

"But it's your last chance to see Marty," I pleaded.

Avery looked as miserable as I felt. "Charlotte," she said. "When we found Marty, I begged you to hide him in the Tower for a few days. You warned me then that you couldn't have pets. 'Just a few days,' I begged. It's been three weeks. That's longer than I ever hoped. And after we plastered the streets with posters, and nobody called, I thought we could keep Marty always. But, Marty has been walked and bathed and loved the whole time, which is a better life than he had in those bushes.

"You don't get it, do you? I'm going to miss Marty like crazy, but that's not totally what I'm upset about."

"It's not?" I said, confused. "Oh, because, I thought ... Well, I mean ..."

"I'm upset because of what you said about the Tower. I know I was the one who ran up into the Tower, before you could stop me.

"But you said it was *ours*, Charlotte," Avery cried, her voice sounding close to tears. "You promised it could be our secret 'apartment' forever. But the Tower wasn't even yours to promise ...

"You lied. You broke one of the new Tower Rules ..."

I started to cry ... She was right .... What could I say?

She picked up Marty one last time, cradling him on his back, and rubbed his belly while he licked her nose.

"I'll come tomorrow to get my stuff," she said, handing me Marty.

CHAPTER 32

Charlotte

MOMENTS OF TRUTH

THE DOORBELL RANG AT SEVEN IN THE MORNING; luckily, my father didn't hear it. My stomach was in such knots. I'd been up since five writing in my journal, but I was still in my pajamas. I threw on a sweatshirt, ran downstairs, and peeked out the living room window. "It's all over," I thought. Mrs. Fields stood on the porch. For a principal to come calling on a Saturday morning at seven, you have to really have messed up. I should have known not to pour out all the stuff about me lying—especially when her granddaughter was one of the ones who had been lied to. She must be coming to have a conference with Dad.

I opened the front door a crack. "Um. My Dad's not awake yet."

"Charlotte," she said, "I'm coming in." She marched through the door and into the front hall. But instead of asking for my Dad, she stopped, closed her eyes and inhaled. "Mmmm, mmmm," she said. "This was a good times house. It even smells the same."

What was she talking about?

"Where did you say that landlady of yours lived?"

Noooo! I thought. She's going to make me apologize to the spooky landlady! Please, no, not that, anything but that. I was positive Dad and I would be history once she heard how I'd invaded *her* Tower and smuggled in a dog.

"Charlotte?" Mrs. Fields looked completely determined. All hope was lost. I could not get out of this.

I pointed to the back of the house.

Mrs. Fields marched ahead while I followed, my hands already trembling, my stomach doing flips. Suddenly, Mrs. Fields yelled so loud I almost jumped out of my skin.

"SAPPHIRE!"

Had she lost her mind? Next she knocked hard on the pantry door. Oh, boy. What if Miss Pierce was a psycho-murderer? I practiced my speech in my head: *I'll never lie again. I learned my lesson. The dog wasn't my idea. Everything will be out by tonight. Please don't kick us out. It wasn't my Dad's fault and I'm just a kid. If you let us stay, I'll never, ever go in your parts of the house again.*

My thoughts were interrupted by a soft voice, "Coming, coming." The pantry door opened, as if by itself.

"Sapphire?" questioned Mrs. Fields. "Where are you?"

"Right here," murmured a quiet voice behind the door.

Mrs. Fields waved us into a room that looked more like the inside of a submarine than a pantry. Lights blinked from two walls lined with a wraparound desk covered with electronic equipment, including a giant flat screen TV and two computer monitors.

Hiding behind the door was a woman just my height wearing jeans and a blue T-shirt. She had a white braid coiled on top of her head. The thing I noticed most were her dazzling, almond-shaped green eyes, as she stared for a moment without speaking. Silence was definitely not a good sign. "I'm sorry ..." I began to stammer.

But before I could get any more words out, Mrs. Fields said, "Sapphire, it's been a very long time."

The little woman didn't say anything. She just dropped her chin.

"Sapphire," said Mrs. Fields. "It's really lovely to see you."

"Ruby ... I ... it's lovely to see you too," said Miss Pierce, looking shyly toward Mrs. Fields.

Mrs. Fields put her hand on my shoulder and looked down at me. "Charlotte, I'd like you to meet my first best friend, Sapphire Pierce."

What was going on?

"Hello," I said, my voice catching in my throat.

"Hello," said Miss Pierce, smiling. "I feel as though I know you a little Charlotte ... I've seen you coming and going many times."

"You have?" I asked, worried.

"That first week, I heard you from your bedroom through the heating vent. I was concerned ... I ... school ... friendships ... except of course for you Ruby ... were difficult for me as well."

"Charlotte," said Mrs. Fields softly. "Sapphire and I were classmates together at a time when being black, or half-chinese like Sapphire, sometimes meant you were excluded. It was a different era. And America was a different kind of country then.

"But Sapphire," Mrs. Fields continued. "What has happened here ... to you ... to my old friend?"

Did I see a brief flash of embarrassment cross Miss Pierce's face before she answered?

"May I offer you both some green tea?" Miss Pierce asked both of us. I nodded emphatically. This was getting good.

Miss Pierce beckoned for Mrs. Fields and me to sit down. She busied herself making tea in a cute little teapot and then served it in those little cups you get in Chinese restaurants—the ones without the handles.

"Ruby, you know that I was a very shy child. Our friendship was so important to me. But, instead of growing out of my shyness as I grew older, I grew more into it. And before I knew it, I just stopped being part of the world. I stuck with my stars. But when you, Charlotte, and your father moved in, I don't know why, but I began to look forward to you coming home. The day you called out that you were home, I almost broke my 12 years of solitude," she said.

"That was you?" I asked. "I knew I heard a voice!"

"I'm sorry," she whispered. "I should have come out. But a twelve-year habit was simply too hard to break."

She looked so nervous; I wanted to make her feel better. "I know all about hard habits to break," I said. "The first day of school I always have a disaster."

Miss Pierce nodded. "I'd just like to say that I am happy that you and your father came to live in my house," she said.

"You are?" I asked. She must not yet know all the rules I'd broken.

"Oh, yes. You've brought friends and laughter and memories to a house that Ruby used to call, 'The Good Times House.' But it hasn't been that for a long, long time." Her green eyes filled up again.

Mrs. Fields comforted her just like she had comforted me and probably hundreds of other kids through the years. "It's quite all right, Sapphire," she said firmly. "You'll see. The good times are coming back. I can feel it."

Miss Pierce smiled through her tears. "I do hope that's true, Ruby," she said. "I did think maybe there were possibilities six weeks ago when the trap door bell rang on a Saturday night."

I gasped. I *knew* that bell in the vent was attached somewhere. That meant she'd heard us every time we opened the Tower!

"Don't worry," said Miss Pierce. "I was so relieved you had found some friends. I liked knowing that children were using the Tower again. And I loved peeking around the porch to see all you girls. But I am curious. How did you discover the switch?"

I answered, "Well, that's a long story."

"Um, Miss Pierce, there is something else I need to tell you," I stammered.

"Yes, I'm all ears." She smiled warmly at me. That gave me confidence to go on.

"Uh, I snuck a dog into your house. It wasn't my idea. It was Avery's, but I went along with it and hid Marty up there and I'm really, really sorry. I know we aren't allowed to have pets. Dad's taking him to the shelter today."

Miss Pierce laughed hoarsely from somewhere deep in her throat—the same laugh I'd heard on the porch just two mornings before. "Oh, Ruby, I wish you could have seen it. I happened to be putting out my grocery list for Yuri when I caught this poor child trying to wrestle a wiggly, grey-and-white mutt into a dress."

"You know about Marty?" I asked.

"Well, yes," she said. "We became acquainted the morning I went upstairs to readjust the digital camera on the telescope. Someone had aimed it."

Digital camera? Miss Pierce in the Tower? Marty and Miss Pierce? My mind was racing. "There's a d-d-digital camera on the telescope?" I stammered in excitement. "Yes," she said. "I've retired from serious research but there's nothing to stop a retired astronomer from trying to discover a new star," she said. "I record pictures every night and study them here on my computer." She led us over to the monitor and brought up an image of the treetops and sky above the house.

"Wow! Where's the digital camera?" I asked.

"You can't see it," said Miss Pierce. "It's built into the telescope and wireless. I've programmed it to take photos every night."

"Every night?" I asked. Suddenly, an embarrassing thought crossing my mind.

"Yes, every night."

"Then you saw ..."

Miss Pierce walked over to one of her computers and clicked on a folder labeled "October 12." Instantly, the screen filled with pictures of Maeve and Nick at Montoya's.

"Sorry," I said.

Miss Pierce laughed. "No matter. It was highly entertaining."

So far, she hadn't said anything about kicking us out of her house. I was so relieved I almost started crying. "Miss Pierce, thank you for understanding. Thank you for letting us stay. Thank you for not being too mad about Marty."

"You're welcome, dear. Have you tried to find his previous owners?"

I nodded. "Avery put up posters everywhere. She even

put a notice on the town website. He had a rabies tag, but it was from New Hampshire and nobody could find the owners. Their phone number was disconnected and there was no forwarding address.

"How sad," said Miss Pierce. "I've never really been a dog person."

"Me neither," I said.

"But I've gotten sort of attached to Marty."

"I know what you mean. Marty is so cute and he is the best snuggler. Sometimes he sleeps under the covers with me and ..." I stopped in mid-sentence. I knew I was beginning to ramble. That was a habit of mine.

"If it hadn't been for that little dog we might not have met today," she continued.

"That's true," I said.

"Charlotte, I don't want this house to be silent anymore," said Miss Pierce. "If your father says it's all right, you can keep Marty. And you girls can use the Tower."

"Really?" I shouted. "Do you mean it? Oh, thank you, Miss Pierce. I jumped up from the table and was about to hug her. But I could see she wasn't ready for that yet. Maybe later.

"Marty won't be any trouble. I promise. Thank you so much. I can't wait to tell Avery! I can't wait to tell Dad. I want Dad to meet you!" I was so excited I couldn't stop talking. I had so many more questions to ask about things like the key and the parchment. But Miss Pierce was looking a little tired.

"Sapphire ... welcome back," said Mrs. Fields, her voice catching. She turned to me. "Charlotte, it's been a big day for all of us, but mostly, I think for Sapphire. I'll come back another day and chat about old times. Charlotte, no doubt you have plans to make?"

"I sure do! Thank you, Miss Pierce. It's so nice to meet

✿
189

you. I promise you won't be sorry I moved in."

Miss Pierce looked at me and smiled ... really smiled. "I don't believe I will Charlotte."

I couldn't wait to tell the girls that Marty and the Tower were ours forever. But I wanted to tell them in a way they'd always remember.

CHAPTER 33

Katani

BREAKING THE NEWS

MY GRANDMOTHER SANG TO SOFT-ROCK the whole way to Charlotte's. Not only was that incredibly embarrassing, but couldn't she see what a tragedy all of this was? Frankly, I was getting really annoyed with her. When we picked up Avery and Maeve, she chatted with them as if we were going to a party. None of us said a word ... not even Maeve. Avery didn't want to be there at all. Even for someone who isn't afraid to stop the hardest kick or snowboard the steepest slope, facing the Tower without Marty was too tough.

"Don't go anywhere, Grandma Ruby. We're gonna move our things out as fast as we can."

"Without running into Charlotte, if possible," added a huffy Maeve.

A note on the door said:

Please come straight up to the Tower.
~ Charlotte

"Hmmph," I snorted.

Sounding depressed Maeve asked, "Couldn't we just go home?"

Grandma Ruby told us to "Be brave" and that she would wait for us.

There wasn't a sound as we headed toward the trap door.

"Let me handle this," I said to the others.

What was that girl up to? I stuck my head through the trap door.

"SURPRISE!" shouted Charlotte.

At the top of the stairs stood Charlotte and Marty. All four windows sparkled but it wasn't just from the late afternoon sun. Charlotte had strung twinkly lights on each window, spelling our names. The Tower looked so beautiful. I was so overwhelmed I couldn't even speak.

CHAPTER 34

Avery

REUNITED

THAT MISCHIEVOUS, FURRY, GRAY-AND-WHITE FACE peeked over the side before I even got to the top of the stairs.

"MARTY! YOU'RE STILL HERE!" He jumped into my arms, licking my face, and barking like a maniac. "What's going on, Charlotte? I thought you were bringing him to the shelter. Do we get to keep him? Do we? Do we? Do we?"

I'll never forget what she answered as long as I live. "He's ours forever, Avery. Marty's here to stay."

CHAPTER 35

Maeve

OUR NAMES IN LIGHTS

THERE ARE THREE THINGS I'VE ALWAYS DREAMED OF: a surprise party, a candlelight dinner with roses on the table, and my name in lights. That day, Ms. Charlotte Elizabeth Ramsey, world traveler and BSG forever, made all three dreams come true. I was the last to reach the Tower. By the time I made it up the stairs, Avery was being licked by Marty. And Katani, who had recovered from her momentary attack of speechlessness, was firing a million questions at Charlotte. The scene in the Tower took my breath away. A table covered with a white lace tablecloth was set with crystal bowls of crème brûlée, which tasted delicious. The centerpiece was divine: gardenias and white roses, my absolute favorite.

And the windows! I don't know how she did it. Hundreds of little lights spelled out our names. Mine was so bright, I was sure everyone west of Summit Avenue would see it. Maybe even Billy Trentini, who is definitely hot!

CHAPTER 36

Charlotte

THE RETURN OF THE BSG

THE GIRLS WANTED TO KNOW EVERYTHING. Katani sat me down in the Lime Swivel and paced around me, asking questions like a television interviewer.

First, I apologized for lying. "If I had just told the truth in the first place, we could have met Miss Pierce and asked to use the Tower so much sooner!" I said. "And then none of this horrible stuff would have happened and we wouldn't have had to sneak around. I promise I'll never lie to you guys again. I just wanted to keep everybody happy, and the lie kept getting worse and worse."

Katani nodded her head wisely then said, "The truth is always the simplest way, Charlotte."

Just what her wonderful grandmother had said, but I didn't let on. I was so happy to be back sitting in the Lime Swivel surrounded by my new best friends, I didn't care how many times I got the same good advice.

"I understand," said Maeve. "The first time I had to leave the class for untimed standardized testing, I told the kids my mother was taking me to meet Madonna."

"Honestly, Maeve," said Katani, with her hands on her hips, while Avery and I giggled.

"The next day everyone was asking for her autograph so I had to sneak and write a bunch of them at recess," Maeve continued to explain.

"Did they believe you?" Avery asked.

"They might have if I hadn't spelled her name 'Madnona.'"

When we stopped laughing, Avery stood up with Marty and said, "After long and careful deliberation, Charlotte, we forgive you." She held Marty toward the chair to give me a doggy kiss.

"Yuck!" I shouted. "Dog slime!"

ᘓ

"What's the old lady who owns the house like?" asked Katani. "Why didn't she ever come out?"

"Is it true she was abandoned at the altar?" asked Maeve.

"No. But I think she did have her feelings hurt a lot when she was kid for being an 'other.' After her parents died, she holed up in the back of the house and rented the second floor to help support herself. She's an astronomer. She'd just rather deal with the stars than with people. She's very, very shy."

Katani nodded in sympathy.

"I felt that way," she said, "when I first noticed kids teasing Kelley. I told Grandma I didn't want to go to school anymore if people were so mean. She gave me such a lecture about how we need to fix our surroundings instead of running away from them. You know my grandmother; I never dared complain again."

"Would you like to meet her?" I asked the girls.

ᘓ

When we walked into the back pantry, Mrs. Fields and Miss Pierce were sipping tea together as naturally as if they did it every night.

Katani looked completely confused.

Mrs. Fields was laughing as she stood up to give Katani a hug. "Sapphire, I'd like you to meet my granddaughter."

"How do you do!" said Miss Pierce, reaching out her hand for a handshake.

"Katani, this is my dearest and best friend from childhood, Sapphire Pierce."

For once, the ever-cool Katani lost it. "You *know* each other? ... No way!"

Miss Pierce's green eyes sparkled. "We've been friends more than 50 years," she said.

"Then how come I never met you?" Katani sputtered.

Miss Pierce's smile faded.

Mrs. Fields coughed and began an explanation but was interrupted.

"It's a long story, Katani," Miss Pierce said in a semi-whisper. "I moved to California for college. Your grandmother was always wonderful about keeping in touch. I wasn't. After a while I stopped writing. When I moved back here twenty years later, it felt too late. And being a shy person, I didn't reach out to the most loyal friend I ever had." She looked a bit sad ... maybe for all the lost years.

"I know what that's like," I said. "You think you're going to stay in touch forever but you don't."

"The important thing is, girls," said Mrs. Fields, "Sapphire and I are back in touch. And we're not going to lose track of each other ever again."

Miss Pierce's shy smile warmed us all.

"Grandma," asked Katani, "did you come to this house

when you were young too?"

Mrs. Fields told the story of how she and Miss Pierce had first met in elementary school and became fast friends, constantly playing at each other's houses.

"Is the lime green swivel chair still in the Tower?" asked a curious Mrs. Fields.

"You know about the chair?" Katani asked.

"Know about it! Your great-grandfather was so proud of that chair ..."

"That was Great-Grandpa's chair!" said Katani.

"Yes, he bought it for his barbershop for some of the ladies to sit in when they came in for their fancy bob haircuts. Grandpa was the only barber in the neighborhood who knew how to do the new Jackie Kennedy bob. He was very courtly and thought the ladies should have a fancy chair."

"Your great-grandfather was one of the best hair stylists in Boston," said Miss Pierce.

"Runs in their family," I said.

Katani was enchanted. "I can't believe I'm using the same chair! How did you get it to the Tower?"

Miss Pierce and Mrs. Fields started laughing, each trying to talk and explain.

"That was a day, Sapphire, wasn't it? Remember telling my grandfather we could move it ourselves?"

"Ha!" laughed Miss Pierce. "By the end of the day, your uncle came over with a friend ..."

"And," continued Mrs. Fields, chuckling, "the two of them got a rope and dragged and pushed it up the stairs while we clapped and cheered them on. Your mother was convinced the chair would fall on someone's head! Remember how she kept admonishing us to sit still? 'You are like bees. You might sting somebody if you keep buzzing about like that.'"

Avery was so excited, she looked like she was going to explode. "If you used to play in the Tower, were you the BSG?"

Miss Pierce nodded. "The Tower was our refuge from the world. We were best friends who wanted a place of our own—away from school, away from family, and away from troubles. As you saw, we made up an oath. We wrote it on a piece of paper long ago."

"Us, too!" chirped Avery. "What does BSG stand for?"

Miss Pierce took a deep breath and began. "Ruby and I spent all our afternoons and weekends going between each other's houses. Beacon Street was the road that connected us. It was my father who named us the Beacon Street Girls. 'You two spend more time running back and forth down Beacon Street than the trolley,'" he said.

Mrs. Fields chuckled.

"My father was a jeweler, and a quiet man," continued Miss Pierce. "He watched my mother's heart break when people snubbed her, so he was especially appreciative of our close friendship. He was always doing special things for me and Ruby. On my twelfth birthday, he gave me a treasure box with a key he crafted himself."

Katani's eyes widened. She looked from Miss Pierce to her grandmother. "The key!" she said.

Mrs. Fields eyes twinkled as she reached up under her turtleneck and pulled out a necklace with an exact replica of the key that she had seen Katani wear.

"You have one too!" said Katani. "No wonder you had that look on your face when you saw it around my neck! I wondered why you kept asking me questions."

"After working at a junior high for forty years, not much surprises me, Katani," she said. "But I have to admit, seeing that key around your neck was quite an emotional experience."

"How did you girls find it?" Miss Pierce asked.

"It was me," said Avery with pride. "I jumped on a floorboard and found it."

"And we know which floorboard, don't we Ruby?" said Miss Pierce.

"We surely do," said Mrs. Fields. "Right up there beside your telescope. I hope you're keeping it in a safe place, Katani. I was so relieved to see you weren't wearing it around your neck any more."

"It's been back under the floorboard since that day, Grandma," said Katani. "I wasn't taking any more chances."

"I've got it," I added. "I was hoping you could tell us about it."

Then I handed the jeweled key to Miss Pierce who examined it proudly.

"I had forgotten how exquisite it was," she said. "My father hand cast the jewels himself. My birthday card said: 'A treasure box to hold the secrets of friendship. For my two gems, Ruby and Sapphire, the Beacon Street Girls.'"

"But where's the treasure box?" asked Katani.

"Where's the treasure?" asked Maeve.

"I'm afraid it was only treasure to us," explained Mrs. Fields. "A glass horse we bought at a fair we went to together ..."

"Tickets to our first movie at the Beacon Street Movie House," continued Miss Pierce.

"That's where I live!" shouted Maeve. "Did you go there in the olden days?"

The two ladies laughed. "Every Saturday for the matinee," said Mrs. Fields.

"Never missed it," said Miss Pierce.

"You have to come back," said Maeve. "You would love the theater now. My parents have restored the balcony and the curtains and the gold decorations."

Miss Pierce shook her head. "I'm afraid I don't much care for new movies. *Singin' in the Rain* and *Gone With the Wind* were more my type. Although I must admit, I did want to see *Star Wars*."

"Miss Pierce," said Maeve, putting her arm around her, "You and I have a beautiful future together."

"Please, Maeve, could we talk about the movies later?" Katani begged. "Think treasure!"

"I removed all our tickets and trinkets from the box years ago," said Miss Pierce.

"But where's the box?" interrupted Avery.

"It's in the Tower," Miss Pierce said softly. She paused. "Waiting to be filled with the treasures of the next Beacon Street Girls."

"Wow! That's us!" said Maeve. "This is better than a Hollywood movie."

"Life is always better than fantasy, dear. It's real," said Mrs. Fields.

"We won't be coming up there," said Miss Pierce. "The Tower is yours now. On your way up, Charlotte, why don't you ask your father down to have tea with us, please. I want to officially welcome him."

"Where's the box?" shouted Avery, crouched like a runner on the starting blocks.

"You know the window that faces Boston and the sea?"

"Charlotte's window!" said Katani.

"Look to the right of it," said Miss Pierce.

We raced upstairs to the Tower.

First, I had to take down the quote from *The Little Prince*. Then, all I could see was a knot hole in the paneling.

"Look," said Maeve.

Typical Avery. She pushed the knot hole, and behind it was the box.

Katani handed me the key.

"It's yours, Charlotte," she said. "You're the one who made it all happen."

"Me?" I asked. "But you planned the first sleepover."

"But if you hadn't zipped the tablecloth in your pants and ruined my top and met my grandmother and made me so mad, I might never have planned it in the first place."

"What about me?" said Avery. "I'm the one who found the bell and jumped on the floorboard and ..."

"Whatever!" groaned Maeve. "Charlotte, if you don't try that key soon, I will."

My hand was shaking when I turned the key to open the box. The girls huddled around.

Katani caught her breath. "It's so beautiful."

"Oooh," said Maeve, touching the velvet inside. "What are you going to put in there, Charlotte?" Maeve asked. "You should be in charge of the first treasure."

I knew exactly what I was going to put in there. I'd been thinking about it ever since Miss Pierce told us about the box. I walked over to my window seat and picked up Mom's denim jacket.

"Too big," giggled Avery. "It'll never fit."

I reached into the pocket and pulled out my dad's new digital camera (this time I had permission). I said, "Ladies, we are going to memorialize this moment."

"Cool," offered up Avery.

"Katani," I asked. Would you mind getting that sign behind the Lime Swivel?"

I could see Avery pointing excitedly at Marty.

"Yes, Avery," I assured her. "Marty can be in the picture. After all he is our official mascot. Maeve, you are in charge of posing us all."

Katani held up the sign as Maeve and Avery cheered and whooped. I have to admit, I was pretty proud of my handiwork. The sign proclaimed "BSGs Forever."

"Charlotte, this is so fabulous," said Maeve. "And look everyone, to top it all off Charlotte put hearts for me; diamonds for you, Katani; we can guess who the soccer balls are for; and most importantly, a big bone with a red ribbon for Mr. Marty. Charlotte, you rule!"

I couldn't help myself. I reached over and gave Maeve a hug. She hugged back.

"OK ..." said Maeve, clapping her hands together like a movie director. "Strike your poses girls, and remember, this is for history."

"Wait a minute," said Katani, who had been staring intently at my work of art. "You forgot something."

I started to panic. I had spent all morning on this sign. "What could I have possibly missed?"

Avery came to my defense. "She did not Katani. This sign looks great. Charlotte thought of everyone, even Marty. You are just being picky."

"Really picky," chimed in Maeve.

This was not going well.

In the meantime, Katani was at my desk. She had pulled out my markers and pencils and had begun to draw something on the sign.

Avery yelled at Katani to stop. Maeve told Avery to be

quiet. And I ... I slumped down in the Lime Swivel, leaned my head back on the chair and closed my eyes. "Would I ever get anything right?" I wondered.

Suddenly, I heard them all yell.

"You forgot the stars!" they shouted in unison.

It was true. I had forgotten to put stars on the sign. But, it was OK. My friends remembered.

"Let's get this movie started," giggled Maeve.

I jumped up and set the timer on the camera. We pulled over a little footstool and Avery arranged Marty on top of a fancy, red velvet pillow. Then she bribed him with a cracker to sit still on top of the stool. We all stood behind Marty, each holding a piece of the sign. Maeve happily ordered us to "Smile for the camera!"

Later when we printed out the picture, Katani made us each cut a lock of our hair to put in the box too. Avery insisted that we put some of Marty's hair in as well. Maeve wasn't totally happy with the way her hair looked in the picture and wanted us to do the picture again. But, Katani told Maeve that because she was a redhead, she would always stand out. Maeve was fine with that.

All in all, a great ending to a pretty great day, I thought. And come to think of it, it was a pretty great beginning too.

EPILOGUE

sophie, ma cherie,
u wont believe this. But everything has
turned out so fine and great and
wonderful. i want u to meet my new
friends someday. I know they will love
you and u will love them. let's never
4get each other. OK? we must find a way
to stay in touch always.
your friend,
charlotte

```
From: Sophie
To: Charlotte
Subject: of course friends

but of course I have not forgotten you,
dear charlotte. I am so glad you have new
friends, but I hope you will still be
mine and not forget me. our teacher this
year is magnifique. we are doing penpals
and I ask him if we can write your class.
you and I could match up the kids! maybe
I write the boy u tell me about, nick.
what do u think? Be sure to ask your
teacher.
Love, sophie
```

On Monday, Ms. Rodriguez announced that our assigned lunch seating was over. "I'm so pleased to see how well you all have bonded over the last eight weeks. After this morning's writing assignment, you may eat anywhere you like."

Everyone cheered, including the four Beacon Street Girls. We knew we would keep eating together anyway but as Avery explained it later, "Who's gonna pass up a chance to yell?"

Once we'd settled down again, Ms. Rodriguez asked us to take out our journals.

"Please," she asked, "reread your first journal entry, your first impression of your lunch group. Then on a separate piece of paper, write what you've learned about your lunch group. How does it compare with your first impression? I will be collecting these."

Second Look at First Impressions
By Charlotte Ramsey

I wasn't in class to write a first-impressions sheet. You remember why. I've learned that when it comes to people, nothing is what it seems. As my friend Avery says, "You can't label people and stuff them into tiny boxes because not one of us fits." For example, in my first journal entry, I wrote that Katani was cold. She's not. She's a marshmallow disguised as a cactus. She'll do anything to protect her family and her friends. I wrote that Avery was hyper. Actually, she's the most focused person I know. When she gets her mind on scoring a basket, or blocking a shot, or changing something she thinks is unfair, there's no stopping her. Then there's Maeve. She thinks she's learning challenged. But I know she's gifted. She can learn a dance, memorize a script, and imitate a voice faster than anyone I've ever met. Sure, I can read a book faster than her, but there's no one who can read people faster. And which skill is really more important? While I'm hiding in a book, Maeve is living out loud, making every moment fun for other people.

In conclusion, my first impression of my three lunch partners was that I would give anything to have them as my friends. I feel exactly the same way today.

ଔ

◆

Excellent observations. You remind me of another Charlotte, from one of my favorite books, Charlotte's Web, *by E.B. White. Like you, that Charlotte was also a "true friend and a good writer." Keep writing ... and I wouldn't be at all surprised to see Charlotte Ramsey as an author in her own right some day.*
Ms. Rodriguez

SCHOOL RULE ASSIGNMENTS

Ms. Rodriguez: Class Files
English 101 Assignment:
If I Could Change a School Rule Letter

My thoughts about overall student
performance:
From the sublime to the absurd!

Reminders:
1. Anna and Joline need guidance
2. Language enrichment for Dillon
3. Betsy—suggest she go to see a comedy
   and write a review
4. Nick M. has a lot to say—must
   encourage him to speak up more

Joline Kaminsky
School Rule Assignment

Dear Ms. Rodriguez:

I can't stand the new locker room rule—"No Body Talk." How ridiculous is that? How are girls our age supposed to manage to get dressed and undressed for gym without making a single little comment about stuff that really matters? Yesterday I got yelled at just because I happened to make a couple of tiny observations about somebody's choice of underwear. I won't say who because that's not appropriate but you get my point. How are people going to learn if you don't let them know that days-of-the-week underpants are NOT cool in seventh grade? Isn't this kind of what peer teaching is all about? Drop this rule—that's what I think. (By the way, if it wasn't for gym class I never would've learned how critical it is to shave your legs. Not to mention the whole deodorant thing. Personally I WELCOME criticism—if there ever is any.)

Sincerely,

Joline Kaminsky

&

Anna McMasters
School Rule Assignment

Dear Ms. Rodriguez:

I just don't get why seventh graders can't have open campus. I happen to have an older sister and an older brother and my mom and dad give me all sorts of privileges. I get to watch "R" rated movies and all that kind of stuff. So why can't I go to Starbucks during study hall? Or at least go down the street and pick up some salad or sushi instead of that gross junk they serve us in the cafeteria? I have to watch how many carbs I eat anyway and there's nothing in that place but lasagna and French fries.

Sincerely,
Anna McMasters

❧

Betsy Fitzgerald
School Rule Assignment

Ms. Rodriguez:

First, I just want to let you know that I think this is just a wonderful assignment. I really mean it. It's so important that we students begin to develop a sense of responsibility. This is something I really want to campaign for when I run for class president. Did I mention that to you yet? I think leadership is really important, especially now that I'm in junior high. It's never too soon to start thinking about these kinds of things. Anyway, I'm actually the sort of person who likes rules. I think they really build character. But one thing that kind of concerns me is that we get study hall AND lunch, and I'm just hoping that everyone can really use study hall to their best advantage. I'm thinking that when I run for class president I might suggest that we start a program called "Study Buddies." That way we can really help each other to get our work done. I hope you like my suggestions!

Sincerely,
Betsy Fitzgerald

Nick Montoya
School Rule Assignment

Dear Ms. Rodriguez:
This is just a small suggestion, but kids like me who have jobs after school sometimes need a little extra time to get homework done. I help my folks out in their bakery and some nights I don't finish work until 8 o'clock.
Sincerely,
Nick Montoya

ଓ

Pete Wexler
School Rule Assignment

Dear Ms. Rodriguez:
My brother's school has big pep rallies before all the football games. I'm not just saying this because I'm really into football, but I think we need more support for sports at this school. Seriously. I kind of like the idea of me and all the other guys jogging into the gym and everybody cheering for us and stuff. I also think football players need extra time off on Fridays to get ready for games. I'm the quarterback on the JV team and I need to really psych myself up for hours before I play. Also, this might be a good time to let you know that every other Friday we play away games, and so I have to miss afternoon classes.
Sincerely,
Pete

ଓ

Dillon Johnson
School Rule Assignment

> *Dear Ms. Rodriguez:*
> *More school dances would be good.*
> *Sincerely,*
> *Dillon*

☙

Robert Worley
School Rule Assignment

> *Dear Ms. Rodriguez:*
> *I don't see why we aren't allowed to swap food at lunch. I am SO sick of tofu salad sandwiches on whole grain bread. If I have to eat one more "Not Dog" I think I'll keel. One of the guys in my lunch group actually LIKES this stuff. If we were allowed, he could have my "Not Dog" and I could actually eat a real roast beef sandwich—meat! On white bread!*
> *Sincerely,*
> *Robert*

☙

To be continued ...

don't miss book 2!

BEACON STREET GIRLS

bad news/good news
by annie bryant

beaconstreetgirls.com

Hey Charlotte!
I hope it's good news!

Sneak Preview!
Bad News/Good News

CHAPTER 1

Charlotte

WISHES AND JINXES

Sunday night, way too late

I know I should be in bed already but I can't seem to fall asleep. Dad came into my room a few minutes ago and found me out on the balcony, searching the sky for the Seven Sisters—seven stars that travel together around the skies. It's the constellation that always makes me think of Mom because it was her favorite. Dad's been working like crazy on his new book and he seemed kind of distracted, but he wanted to kiss me good-night and catch up on how things are going. Dad and I have always been close—we have so many inside jokes. Like one of us will say, "Well ... there's good news and bad news. Which do you want to hear first?" And we always answer together, right at the same time, "Give me the bad news first!" I don't know why, but that always cracks us both up.

When Dad asked me what was coming up for this week, I had a whole list. It's hard to believe that just a few weeks ago, I was brand new here and worried that I was going to have to suffer through seventh grade in a new city without a single friend. When I think back on everything that's happened—meeting Maeve,

Avery, and Katani ... all the stuff that we went through before the four of us became such good friends—I feel like the luckiest girl on earth. I'm still not sure what kind of magic turned us from worst enemies into best friends. But it happened, and tonight I feel like Maeve, Katani, Avery, and I are part of a new constellation. Like four stars traveling around together!

I know I'm getting too big to wish on stars. But, it's something I started doing with Mom when I was really young. We'd sit outside together until we could see the first star come out. Then we'd trade wishes. She always said the same thing: My wish is for your wish to come true.

That seems like such a long time ago. I was only four when she died. But even though I'm almost 13 now, wishes still matter. And I ... finally feel at home. That's why, when I saw the first star tonight, I made a wish. Know what it was?

Let this last. Don't let anything change how perfect things are right now.

Ș

Later, thinking back on it, Charlotte decided that all of the trouble had started with her journal entry. *It's as if I knew somehow,* she thought. *It was a jinx. I must have sensed it was all too good to be true.*

worst enemies/best friends Book Extras

- Book Club Buzz
- New Tower Rules
- Amendments
- Trivialicious Trivia
- Charlotte's Word Nerd Dictionary

Book Club Buzz

1. Have you ever faced challenges similar to the hurdles Charlotte encounters as the new girl at Abigail Adams Junior High?

2. Does anyone go out of their way to make Charlotte's first day a little less scary?

3. In *Worst Enemies/Best Friends*, many of the characters find inspiration from different sources: quotations, books, friends, the Tower room, and the stars. What inspires you?

4. Why is the Tower room special for each of the girls?

5. What is the biggest obstacle for the Beacon Street Girls in terms of becoming friends?

more *worst enemies/best friends* Book Club Buzz at beaconstreetgirls.com

The New Tower Rules
Created by The Newest Order
of The Ruby and The Sapphire

Be it resolved that all girls are created equal!

1. We will always speak our minds, but we won't be like obnoxious or anything.
2. We won't put ourselves down, even if we aren't super-smart, super-coordinated, or a supermodel.
3. We'll be loyal to our friends and won't lie to them even if they make a mistake or do something totally embarrassing.
4. We will go for it—how will we know what we can do if we don't try?
5. We will try to eat healthy and stay active. How can you chase your dream if you can't keep up?
6. We won't just take from people and the planet. We'll try to give back good things too.

1. We can all add as many amendments as we like.
2. We will dare to be fashion individualistas—like we're all different so why should we dress the same?
3. Sometimes we'll veg out—just because we feel like it!
4. We should try to save money so if we ever want to, we can start a business or something someday.
5. We should have as much fun as we can.

worst enemies/best friends **trivialicious trivia**

1. What does Charlotte keep in the pocket of her mom's old denim jacket?
   A. journal
   B. charm bracelet
   C. favorite pen
   D. Truffles the Pig

2. What makes Charlotte's First Day Lunchtime Fiasco particularly messy?
   A. spaghetti sauce
   B. fruit punch
   C. grape jelly
   D. syrup

3. What is the name of Kelley's favorite stuffed animal?
   A. Mr. Bear
   B. Miss Mouse
   C. Miss Piggy
   D. Molly

4. Whose family owns the Movie House in Brookline?
   A. Charlotte's
   B. Katani's
   C. Nick's
   D. Maeve's

5. What kind of stationery does Charlotte use to write to her Parisian friend Sophie?
   A. pink with purple flowers
   B. barf bags
   C. school notebook paper
   D. fancy monogrammed C*E*R paper

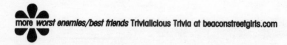
more *worst enemies/best friends* Trivialicious Trivia at beaconstreetgirls.com

6. Where is the secret passage to the Tower?
   A. the bathroom
   B. the ceiling
   C. Charlotte's room
   D. Mr. Ramsey's room

7. What kind of stones are in the silver key that the BSG find in the Tower?
   A. emerald and ruby
   B. diamond and sapphire
   C. ruby and sapphire
   D. garnet and amethyst

8. When does Maeve get the idea for her blanket project?
   A. when she is curled up in her bed at home
   B. during her date with Nick
   C. on the first day of school
   D. right after her date with Nick

9. Miss Pierce is a retired ...
   A. astronomer
   B. English teacher
   C. construction worker
   D. dentist

10. Who was the original owner of the lime green swivel chair?
    A. Miss Pierce
    B. Katani's great-grandfather
    C. Mrs. Fields
    D. Mr. Ramsey

Charlotte Ramsey

Charlotte's Word Nerd Dictionary

BSG Words

Houseboat: (p. 4) noun—a flat-bottomed boat used as a floating home

Laughingstock: (p. 26) noun—a person or thing that is the object of ridicule or teasing

Penetrate: (p. 32) verb—to pass into or through something

Ravishing: (p. 35) adjective—extremely beautiful or attractive

Awestruck: (p. 37) adjective—filled with wonder and admiration

Horrendous: (p. 39) adjective—horrible; dreadful

Gargoyle: (p. 42) noun—a carved figure of a human or an animal, often strange and ugly

Cringe: (p. 44) verb—to shrink or crouch in fear or embarrassment

Turret: (p. 65) noun—a small tower

Detest: (p. 68) verb—to hate or dislike very much

Arboretum: (p. 77) noun—an area where trees are grown for study and display

Gizmo: (p. 95) noun—informal word for a gadget

Primly: (p. 103) adverb—precisely or properly; prissily
Sheepish: (p. 104) adjective—embarrassed or meek
Flail: (p. 142) verb—to swing one's arms and legs wildly
Commotion: (p. 143) noun—intense activity or agitation
Blubber: (p. 161) verb—to make a lot of noise while crying
Traipse: (p. 166) verb—to walk slowly or aimlessly
Cowardly: (p. 175) adjective—without courage
Queasy: (p. 178) adjective—uneasy, uncomfortable, ill
Stammer: (p. 187) verb—to speak with pauses and repetitions
Deliberation: (p. 196) noun—careful consideration and discussion
Admonish: (p. 198) verb—to caution, advise against, or scold
Exquisite: (p. 200) adjective—particularly beautiful, charming, delicate, or refined
Memorialize: (p. 202) verb—to preserve the memory of a person or event

~

Definitions adapted from *Webster's Dictionary*, Fourth Edition, Random House.

BEACON STREET GIRLS

Collect all the BSG books today!

Worst Enemies/Best Friends ☐ **READ IT!**
Yikes! As if being the new girl isn't bad enough ... Charlotte just
made the biggest cafeteria blunder in the history of Abigail
Adams Junior High.

Bad News/Good News ☐ **READ IT!**
Charlotte can't believe it. Her father wants to move away again,
and the timing couldn't be worse for the Beacon Street Girls.

Letters from the Heart ☐ **READ IT!**
Life seems perfect for Maeve and Avery ... until they find out that
in seventh grade, the world can turn upside down just like that.

Out of Bounds ☐ **READ IT!**
Can the Beacon Street Girls bring the house down at Abigail
Adams Junior High's Talent Show? Or will the Queens of Mean
steal the show?

Promises, Promises ☐ **READ IT!**
Elections for class president are underway, and the Beacon
Street Girls are right in the middle of it all. The drama escalates
when election posters start to disappear.

Lake Rescue ☐ **READ IT!**
Big time fun awaits the Beacon Street Girls and the rest of the
seventh grade. The class is heading to Lake Rescue in New
Hampshire for outdoor adventure.

Freaked Out ☐ READ IT!
The party of the year is just around the corner. What happens when the party invitations are given out ... but not to everyone?

Lucky Charm ☐ READ IT!
Marty is missing! The BSG begin a desperate search for their beloved doggie mascot which leads them to an unexpected and famous person.

Fashion Frenzy ☐ READ IT!
Katani and Maeve head to New York City to experience a teen fashion show. They learn the hard way that fashion is all about self-expression and being true to one's self.

Just Kidding ☐ READ IT!
Spirit Week at Abigail Adams Junior High should mean fun and excitement. But when mean emails circulate about Isabel and Kevin Connors, Spirit Week takes a turn for the worse.

Ghost Town ☐ READ IT!
The BSG are off to a real Montana dude ranch for a fun-filled week of skiing, snowboarding, cowboys, and celebrity twins ... plus a ghost town full of secrets.

Also ... Our New **Special Adventure Series:**

Charlotte in Paris ☐ READ IT!
Something mysterious happens when Charlotte returns to Paris to search for her long lost cat and to visit her best Parisian friend, Sophie.

Maeve on the Red Carpet ☐ READ IT!
Film camp at Maeve's own Movie House is oh-so-fabulous. But is Maeve's new friend, Madeline Von Krupcake the star of the Maddiecake commercials, really as sweet as the cakes she sells?

Freestyle with Avery ☐ READ IT!
Avery Madden can't wait to go to Telluride, Colorado to visit her dad! But there's one surprise that Avery's definitely not expecting.